CITY OF GATES

CITY OF GATES

JANICE ELLIOTT

Hodder & Stoughton
LONDON SYDNEY AUCKLAND

Acknowledgement: the author is indebted for the carp of Urfa to John Romer's *Testament* (Michael O'Mara Books, 1988).

British Library Cataloguing in Publication Data
Elliott, Janice
    City of gates.
    I. Title
    823[F]

ISBN 0-340-57115-2

Published by Hodder and Stoughton,
a division of Hodder and Stoughton Ltd,
Mill Road, Dunton Green, Sevenoaks, Kent TN13 2YA
Editorial Office: 47 Bedford Square, London WC1B 3DP

Typeset by Hewer Text Composition Services, Edinburgh
Printed in Great Britain by Biddles Ltd, Guildford and King's Lynn

133841

APR 27 2002

FICTION

Pray for the peace of Jerusalem: they shall prosper that love thee. Peace be within thy walls, and prosperity within thy palaces.

Psalms 122:6–7

ONE

So they came to Jerusalem, pilgrims all in one way or another. There were those simply returning to the Land, as Israel was known to them, and still to them each homecoming felt like a pilgrimage. There were those of other faiths, seeking their god and his monuments. And some, like Daisy Herbert, of little faith but great hope for something she could not have named.

Daisy had a thin skin that freckled, grey eyes, slim bones that gave a false impression of frangibility, and flaming red hair. Not ginger, not golden, but a real red that would hold its light when the sun went in.

On the El Al flight from London to Jerusalem she was sitting next to a grandmother from Tel Aviv.

'You have such beautiful hair, my dear.'

'Thank you. It's awful when it rains though.'

Daisy smiled. The grandmother had been in London, shopping at Marks & Spencer. She said they had M & S in Israel but England was much better. She went every autumn for the jumpers.

She had, in fact, been talking ever since they left London, not just to Daisy. Everyone seemed so friendly, exchanging photographs of their children and grandchildren, calling across the aisle and down the plane. Now they were wishing each other a happy New Year. New Year, Daisy wondered, and then remembered: the Jewish New Year, of course, September.

'And tell me, where are you staying in Jerusalem?'

'Somewhere called Madame Muna's. My cousin Barbara booked. She was meant to be coming but she cancelled. I don't suppose you've heard of it?'

'Oh, yes! Everyone's heard of Madame Muna's.'

At that moment the stewardess came round with boiled sweets and hot towels. She said they would be landing in ten minutes. Daisy's friend said: 'I wonder, my dear, if you'd mind holding my hand? Up I like but not going down.'

When the seat-belt sign went on, Thomas Curtis sighed with a mixture of relief and apprehension. He disliked flying, was suspicious of abroad, wished himself home already, and had begun to forget why he had ever set out. All he could have said was that Jerusalem had flung out a rope of gold and hauled him in.

He edged away from the Israeli child who had kicked his shins all the way from Heathrow, shifted his long legs and practised breathing.

Bad at people, Daisy decided, as for the first time the man across the aisle looked her way. English or possibly east-coast American, she had guessed early on. He had a long neck. She liked his wrists and his profile. Dry? Desiccated? Lonely? The man was out of place anyway on this airborne talking shop. When they landed all the Israelis clapped.

They collided at the exit from the plane. Thomas bumped his head. 'Sorry,' he said.

At the immigration security controls Daisy found herself next to him again. She read the label on his battered suitcase.

'You're going to Madame Muna's too. We could share a taxi? Unless you're being met?'

'Er. Yes. I mean, no.'

Then someone pushed between them and Daisy did not see him again. Perhaps he was lost in the field of folk milling around for taxis, coaches, families. Perhaps he had run away. She waited five minutes but her driver was getting restless.

'We'd better go,' she said.

The man from the plane, she guessed, would be hard to pin down. She would put him out of her mind.

Then it was dusk and her cab was climbing, leaving behind the suburbs of Tel Aviv, up and away into the conifer-scented darkness. She had expected desert, broken hills, arid land, but here, already, was a miracle – each side of the bumpy, winding road was hedged by trees. And by something else she could only just make out in the moonlight.

She leaned forward to speak to the driver.

'What are those stones?'

In the mirror, she could see the driver pull a face. He did not like the question. He shrugged it off.

'The stones of the dead.'

'You mean graves?'

'The fallen. In war. But look. You see?'

Now he was beaming and showing Daisy where to look. And as she glanced up, there, where the night sky should have been, was one bright star, then another, then another.

She understood what he was trying to tell her, what made him laugh as though he were showing her something miraculous, what she was seeing: Jerusalem.

Although to the individuals concerned in this story, their modest destinies would appear to have been worked out in a sequential way, Eugenia Muna, who kept the guest-house by the Jaffa Gate, could have told them that for Jerusalem all times are one, here the first may also be the last of days. So, in company, her enemies gathered, those who would take this City within the walls for bride: Saddam and Nebuchadnezzar, Sennacherib and Allenby, Titus.

Eugenia only had to squint a little and she could see David, weeping, barefoot, in flight from Jerusalem, and hear again the cries of the slaughtered by the hands of Robert of Normandy and Godfrey of Lorraine, Tancred and Raymond of Toulouse.

And then she saw old Moses on Mount Nebo, shading his eyes in the midday heat to catch a shaking image of the city he would never enter. Then he died and was buried in an unmarked grave, and it was dark.

Accordingly, in the Moabite hills, it was to Joshua the children of Israel turned, in question and fear, their eyes dazzled by a star of great brilliance that shot soundlessly across the sky, turned suddenly into an exploding flower of rose and gold, and fell to earth.

Some believed it was the angry spirit of the dead patriarch.

9

Others, that the bones of Joseph they carried to bury in Sechem that is also Nablus, had given them a sign they could not understand.

Joshua could not answer them. He was impatient to get on. There had been enough omens and he could smell goat cooking.

'Go to sleep,' he said. 'You will have forgotten by morning.'

And so they did.

Eugenia knew, this was no shooting star but a Patriot anti-missile missile intercepting a SCUD.

There were occasions when she could have done without information she had never called for and could not use. She had learned early, in her remarkable career through the many loops of time, that knowledge is not wisdom.

But she had no choice in the matter. For in Jerusalem it is forever one time and all times: past, present and to come.

TWO

There are stories in Jerusalem that Madame Muna has been there for ever, in the guest-house behind the goldsmith's, just inside the Jaffa Gate. In her cups (that is frequently, though she holds her liquor amazingly) she will even tell of witnessing Kaiser Wilhelm's arrogant entry on a white horse. For that they had to build a second gate. Only conquerors come mounted.

Eugenia Muna claims to have seen the building of the gate, along with the walls of the City, by Suleiman.

Her companion, Fedor, frequently confused by Eugenia's wilder memories, gets the gates muddled and is convinced that she saw Christ himself come in.

'No,' said Eugenia, not for the first time. 'That was through the Golden Gate, the way by which he will also return.'

'But it's bricked up.'

'Disregarding brick. It is foretold that the kosher Messiah and the Moslem one too, will come the same way on the Day of Judgement.'

'And if they all arrive at the same moment?' Fedor never tires of asking Madame Muna, though never really in the hope of tripping her up, for her answer is always the same.

'Then, obviously, they will come to some arrangement. It is even possible they may all turn out to be one and the same. That would leave a lot of people with fish on their faces.'

Madame Muna puffed with satisfaction, finished jointing the goat and sank into the rocking-chair to read the paper. She wore sheepskin boots and a Manchester United football scarf.

While Madame Muna rocked and read him snippets from the newspaper, Fedor pottered and wiped and scoured.

He had forgotten for how long he had loved Eugenia Muna. He knew that some were sorry for him and considered him exploited. But what did they know of passion such as his? Of the day when he smelled hyacinths between her breasts and saw her wreathed in collared-doves? When he was seized for ever until death by the sight of her instep as she stepped into a *calèche*.

Although he could not remember where this happened – Istanbul? Cairo? Beirut? – Fedor still found himself short of breath when he recalled the fine blue tracing of veins, the perfectly turned heel, revealed in the immortal second when the evening sandal slipped from Eugenia's foot, and he picked it up and gave it back to her.

'Fedor, my dear, that is the second time you have washed the same pan. Now, remind me. The new arrivals?'

'Some cancellations, of course, though we may still have the usual sort of Holy Land package: nuns, an Englishwoman and a Caucasian male who may or may not be attached to her. He could be an archeologist. He has an appointment with the Reverend Pooley.'

'Ah yes, probably to do with the so-called find at the Garden Tomb. Poor deluded souls. Any moment this absurd city may go pouf for the last time. And still they go on digging and arguing. No wonder Jesus wept. Well, we must put on our skates, Fedor. I think a few herbs and a litre of red Carmel with the goat and we can call it lamb, don't you?'

Fedor was still distracted, and not only by thoughts of love.

'Things are hotting up, don't you think?'

Eugenia Muna put aside the *Jerusalem Post* and reached for her pots of spices and bunches of herbs.

Fedor went on: 'You might say they are critical. Both the rabbi and the imam are worried about their families.'

Madame Muna nodded. She looked over her spectacles through the open door to the garden, where, in warm weather, her guests ate out of doors. Her only permanent resident had a great fondness for it.

'There's Miss Mary in the garden. I wish she would get out more. Well, she has green fingers and I suppose that's a blessing. I imagine you'll be going to Magdalena's tonight?'

Fedor nodded. Eugenia Muna pulled a face.

'Queer-looking goat. Do you think they sent us dog?'

Rabbi Solomon and Hamil Ibn Abbas Sartawi, a very minor imam, were Fedor's regular cronies. It was an unlikely friendship across religious divides, and all the more precious for that. Every Thursday they met at Magdalena's, a secret café deep inside the Old City. Tourists never found the shabby door and the corridor cut in the rock. So only the *habitués* knew of the small, calm garden within, or of the fact that behind the bar and up the stairs was housed one of the most ancient brothels in Palestine: first established, it was said, in that brief blink of history when the Crusaders ruled Jerusalem.

Just another instance, old Solomon remarked dryly, of the way in which possession of this battered bride of Christ seemed to inflame every organ from the brain to the crotch.

Solly always made this kind of remark, Fedor suspected, when he was working out a chess gambit. It must be true enough though, that, as Solly said, these few dusty hectares had, through the course of history, despatched more souls to eternity than Hitler himself.

When ruffled, disturbed or in any way anxious, Fedor often turned his inner eye to Magdalena's and the companionship between the three of them that had miraculously survived the violent fortunes of this city. Then he would see them, as through a window: under the vine at the table in the corner of the courtyard. Hamil would be drinking Turkish coffee; Solly preferred Russian tea and Fedor sometimes tea, sometimes a fiery white liquid of dubious origin, known among the regulars as angel's pee.

Fedor realised that beside the other two, heavy with office as they were, he cut an insubstantial figure. Nipping tonight up the steps through the souk that led to the Holy Sepulchre, he had been aware, as often before, of his thinness that was

13

just on the edge of invisibility, his dark suit, greasy with time and service as waiter and washer-up. He sighed when he remembered how once, in another life, and another country, when it was his job to partner lonely matrons at tea-dances among the palms, this suit had been brand new and positively snappy. And he himself had been what might be called groomed. Not that he ever admitted to having performed the services of a gigolo. All the same, he would take the greatest care in those days to shower and powder his body before going to work, to slick down his starling-black hair with Vaseline and to polish his dancing pumps. His cheek, should a partner wish to lay her own against it, would be smooth and sweet as blossom.

This evening, he had nicked himself twice while shaving and arrived at Magdalena's still wearing two blobs of cotton wool.

'My dear friends, I am sorry I am late. Another incident. The road was blocked.'

Hamil nodded but did not comment. Or not directly. There was a tacit agreement between the three that politics as a topic of conversation should be avoided, which may have been one of the reasons their friendship survived. Lately, it had become increasingly difficult to maintain this convention. No one said but all knew that by simply meeting, Abdul and Solly were risking retribution, each from their own people.

From under his heavy lids Hamil continued a scrutiny of the table, into which chess squares had been carved, it was said, even before the second fall of Jerusalem. Hamil and Solly had been playing, intermittently, the same game for three weeks now. Fedor, who had only just reached 'End Game' in his paperback edition of *Play Chess Now*, was more often an observer than a participant. The trouble was, he was distracted by the enchantment of the language and the beauty of the light ebony and weighty onyx pieces. A battle of giants! Of kings and queens and bishops and knights, commanding armies of pawns, all served or ruthlessly wiped from the board by that stealthy warrior the rook, who was not a bird but a castle. Last night when he had at last got to bed he had resumed his study of the King and Pawn v King

14

end game, only to lose himself in the enticing mysteries of the magic square which, like so much of life, was not real until you imagined it.

Without raising his eyes from the table-top, the imam said: 'I hear the Christians are losing their hospice next door.'

Solomon looked up. His gaze was more open, always darting.

'Kalfayan the Armenian again?'

'So I understand.' Hamil's voice was hoarse from his early years as a muezzin, five times a day calling the faithful to prayer and prostration. 'That man is the true dirt in this city. He is the manipulator. Through his agents Moslem sells to Moslem but they are tricked. It is your people who buy. Not that I hold you to account, my friend. The Prophet himself was troubled by Satan.'

Fedor held his breath. He could never decide if his two friends were the greatest of saints or the profoundest of cynics, that they could not only meet like this but maintain what appeared to be some degree of detachment, while everywhere beyond the walls of Magdalena's the bloody confrontation between their two armies of God grew each day more clamorous. So this city of bells and prayers and pilgrims and beauty and ancient filth was filled with one great shout of hatred.

It was here, perhaps, that Fedor had some small role to play. There were times, when the air across the table crackled, that one or the other would take the initiative; abandoning the board they would turn to their other game: the telling of tales of love. Carnal or divine – it was no matter. But one thing was certain: Fedor was both umpire and initiator. His tales were not necessarily the best but both imam and rabbi depended upon him to start them off.

Fedor had hoped today to witness Solly's long-promised exposition of the Byzantine ploy, an end game the rabbi claimed to have learned as a child from the lips of a secret grandmaster in the time of the holocaust, when, unknown to the rest of the world, the most extraordinary chess-game in history, and the most dangerous, was played in and between the death-camps and ghettos.

Solly still refused to reveal by what mysterious telegraph, knight in Bergen-Belsen took queen's pawn in Auschwitz. Or how men so reduced could summon the mental energy to play at all.

'Ah,' Solly would say, 'this was our defiance, our resistance. In here!' And he would tap his skull, then bend over the table, gathering the other two to listen. 'At one time there were no less than fifty games in progress all over Europe. Necessarily there was a turnover in players, but as one fell out another took his place.'

'Why are you whispering?' Hamil said. 'There is no need to whisper now.'

'That's what you think,' Solly said.

After all, tonight Fedor was not required to tell a story. Solly and Hamil Ibn Abbas Sartawi were united in their dislike of the Armenian.

'One hears,' said Hamil, cracking his long yellow fingers, 'that Kalfayan has more diseases than a dog. Than an Iranian dog,' he added.

'Of a social nature?' Solly's eyes were bright.

'Naturally.'

'Magdalena says he can no longer make love,' Fedor offered. The other two looked mildly startled, as though they had forgotten that Fedor was there. Sometimes he felt like the dormouse in *Alice in Wonderland*.

'Well, Magdalena should know.' Fedor always enjoyed Solly's ample laugh. Up went his hands, his whole body laughed. Fedor would hear in his sleep now and then, that wonderful laugh, feel the bed shake. As laughter went it was on the cosmic scale: magnificent, billowing, bellowing, a summons to joy as peremptory as Jerusalem's less kindly clamour. God was right about the children of Israel. They were stiff-necked. A pity he'd never heard Solly laugh. Or perhaps he had?

'Who's talking about me?'

At that moment Magdalena came out of the bar and down the steps to the courtyard. Trying to forget that one of Madame Muna's few weaknesses was her jealousy of Magdalena, Fedor observed, with an almost objective

16

pleasure, the sway of her hips, the way her superb breasts joined in this interesting movement.

'And what were you saying?'

Fedor actually blushed as Magdalena rested one hand on his shoulder, the other on her hip. It was said she modelled herself on Sophia Loren when young but Fedor felt it should have been the other way round, if there were any justice in the world. Although they shared a predicament, that neither Fedor nor Magdalena knew where they came from, this was a problem she had dismissed as casually as a bird, forgetful of the egg from which it had been hatched.

Her real name was not even Magdalena. It was simply a tradition that the name went with the café and always had.

So the evening had passed, from dusk into night. Magdalena sat with them a while, openly firting with Solly, bringing a glitter to Hamil's eye and teasing Fedor. She spoke of Kalfayan ('that rubbish!') and spat with brilliant precision into the basin of the small fountain at the centre of the courtyard.

She scratched her unshaved legs and as she bent to kiss him goodnight on the cheek, Fedor reeled at the delicious odour of her armpits: sweat, cardamom, musk, and essence of Magdalena herself. Never would he have been unfaithful to his beloved Eugenia Muna. All the same, he had to cross his legs and only breathed easily again when she was obliged to escort a personal customer upstairs. When the light in the room above the bar came on Fedor averted his eyes and downed his angel's pee, calling for another.

The three friends sat on for another half hour. There was the familiar yip yip of the security police van on the road to Damascus, a distant bang and a crackle of what might have been gunfire or fireworks.

But for once the Old City itself was not ripped by alarms. Doubtless the Temple Faithful were planning yet another assault on the Mount, plotting to lay the foundation stone from which would rise a third temple. But for this evening at least, the three could sit around their table and talk or be silent in peace.

The heavy silver stars came out and Hamil named them. 'They are more beautiful in the desert,' he said. And in his rasping voice went on to tell Solly and Fedor how when he was very young and living in Nablus ('higher even than Jerusalem') a bird had come down from a tree and told him to go on the hajj to Mecca. It had accompanied him all the way, although no one else had seen it: perched in the bows of the vessel in which he crossed the Red Sea.

'And then it was with me to the sacred stone itself. I have told no one else in the world of this for it would be idolatrous, a great sin. But I still wonder. It was a black, ragged bird. It comes to me in my sleep and I wonder, is it a fakir, a djinn or Allah himself? It is true that ravens with stones in their beaks came to the assistance of the prophet Mohamet in one of his battles. All the same, I must ask you never to speak of this.'

The other two shook their heads.

Then it was time to part. Magdalena had shushed out her last customer. They had turned off the lights in the bar and the candles in the courtyard guttered in a night breeze.

'Next week,' each said as they always did. Trotting home, Fedor realised that Solly had still not revealed the Byzantine ploy. Perhaps he never would? Perhaps that was the ploy?

He swore he could find his way through this city with his eyes shut. All the same, he hurried, taking care not to give the appearance of hurry, and he looked neither to right nor left as he nipped down the Way of the Cross.

THREE

*I*n his flat looking on to the Garden Tomb and the bus station, the Reverend Morgan Pooley was supposed to be doing a number of things. Instead, he was playing with his small cat Sheba, eating tinned quails from his mother's Christmas hamper (rather boring), wondering whether to part his hair on the other side, worrying about love and if he would ever fall in it, remembering his happy days as a fag at a minor English public school that had failed to catch on to the new emancipation, running through his list of things to do and at the same time marvelling at the number of concerns, large and small, that could be contained within one very average head at one moment.

He crumpled his preliminary list into a ball and threw it for Sheba to stalk. Then he looked in the mirror and saw what he always saw: a fair-haired Englishman with potentially laughing blue eyes and nothing at all written on his face.

Then Morgan started his list all over again.

It read:

Make list re drinks: lumpfish?
B. Banks' cousin: note
Ring Jesus Tours re Tomb closed
Letter Mother
Hay & Windo – deadline *no way*
Sheba flea-collar
Scotch House polo shirt
Gas mask?

Morgan sighed. He knew the feeling so well. Writing a list tidied life up into something manageable for about five minutes. Well; maybe for twelve hours or so, provided you left it where it was and did not touch it, you felt almost as though you might come back and find everything magically done.

What really happened was that the list got lost or the cleaner moved it or new contingencies made it out of date.

Morgan poured himself a glass of Celebration Cream. He drank the disgusting stuff, he decided, because it reminded him of the cough-mixture matron used to dole out in the san. As he drank, he managed at the same time to scribble the note to the Banks woman's cousin (he saw her as a Banks clone, plain and bossy) and to ponder the amazing vitality of the fantasy life. Here he was in Jerusalem (itself a fantasy, in a way), a nervy city anticipating its likely umpteenth fall, bristling with unpleasant weapons, heart- and head-sick with politics, hopeless for shopping.

And yet although he was here he was not here but in another Jerusalem where his sole duty was as guardian to that quiet tomb below his window. In this Jerusalem of Morgan's dreams there were no package tours. His duties as guide were called upon only now and then, for the benefit of an occasional charming and discriminating academic. No flat-chested Englishwomen with peeling noses demanding Communion. No shop to supervise. No Israel. No bangs in the night. No traffic jams. No traffic. No Bishop. In particular no Bishop's wife, force-feeding him her dreadful spotted dick. Plenty of time for the water-colours which had been admired as not so far from David Roberts.

Ah well. At least the closing of the Tomb and the present emergency had freed him from his job as guide. So there was time too for the Hay & Windo commission for a would-be popular work provisionally entitled Love and the Bible. There was to be particular reference to Jerusalem and the Old Testament.

Morgan had undertaken the job blithely enough. The only problem was that researching and writing a book was turning out to be a permanent and spasmodically pleasant condition. Sitting, as he was now, at his desk, with the green-shaded lamp at his elbow and Sheba tiptoeing over his papers, Morgan felt happy.

Since to finish this work would mark the end of this happiness, he had sensibly decided to put off for as long as possible – perhaps forever – the completion and delivery of the book. It had thus been a nasty moment when his editor, Ms Barbara Banks, announced that she would be arriving in Jerusalem, a profound relief when she cancelled. The commission money was in his Abbey National Sterling Asset account. He might in the end have to hand it back but if he could only prevaricate for a couple more years it would have clocked up a nice little interest.

Morgan filled his glass, put out of his mind the wasp-shaped worry that B. Banks might have sent her cousin to spy on him, reached for his box-file of notes and for his pre-NEB school Bible: a volume he could never touch without a frisson of nostalgia for he knew not what. Surely he could not have enjoyed ice-cold showers and the swish of the cane?

He had talked about this once to Eugenia Muna, who was one of his favourite people in Jerusalem. But all she had said was: 'I suppose someone has to be English. I have always felt myself that it is an island fit only for sheep.'

Morgan turned to the page of notes he had headed in his precise italic script: Sacred or Profane? Rabbi Akiva and the Song of Songs – the making of the Hebrew Bible at Jamnia, first century AD. The Song had so nearly been lost. Akiva had let it stay but forbade its singing in beer-halls. For the old rabbi as for King James's men, the song was the great image of, in the one case God's, in the other Christ's, love for Jerusalem.

And yet, and yet. My beloved is white and ruddy, the chiefest of ten thousand. His head is as the most fine gold, his locks are bushy and black as a raven.

I charge you, O daughters of Jerusalem, if ye find my beloved, that ye tell him, that I am sick of love.

Morgan shook his head. The truth was, he was most deliciously, mysteriously and guiltily stuck with his vision of Solomon's sweet-voiced love, leaping upon the mountains, skipping upon the hills.

Could Akiva, that stiff-necked puritan, have got it wrong? Or was he, Morgan Pooley, the most wicked of interpreters (though not the first) to find himself dizzy with a longing that had nothing to do with Jerusalem, reading the words he had no need to read, since he had them by heart?

Stay me with flagons, comfort me with apples: for I am sick of love. His left hand is under my head and his right hand doth embrace me.

Sheba rubbed her back against his wrist and Morgan read on: Rise up, my love, my fair one, and come away. He scratched the little cat under her chin.

As the shadows gathered in the garden below and Jerusalem held its breath after the heat of the day and before the alarms of the night, Morgan began to hum and Sheba to purr.

Daisy unpacked by the light of a candle. The moment they had reached the outskirts of the City all those lights she had mistaken for stars went out, and Jerusalem was extinguished.

Arriving near midnight at Madame Muna's, she had been received by a small man remarkable only for his shaving scars. It was he who had produced the candle, led her to her room, offered a sandwich and apologised for the power cut.

'Are you busy?' she asked.

'Not so much.' Fedor shook his head. 'The troubles, you know. But tomorrow we expect Pilgrim Tours.' He hovered. Daisy wondered if he might be waiting for a tip but she sensed not. Then he said: 'And you? You are on holiday? Or perhaps it is work?'

Daisy smiled. The little man touched her.

'I'm just a tourist. Looking for the Holy Land, I suppose.'

'Ah, yes.'

'Perhaps you could help me, when I've settled in.'

'My pleasure.'

Fedor gave a stiff little inclination of the head and left, closing the door quietly.

Daisy heard a cab draw up, a door slam, and, soon after, feet on the stairs. The man from the plane, she guessed.

In his room, Thomas sat on the edge of his bed. He was glad of the power cut. By the light of the candle the simple room, with its whitewashed walls and lack of decoration, could have been a pilgrim cell.

He patted the bed. Hard. Good.

He stood. Nothing to unpack really but he laid out shaving things, scratched his stubble and wondered whether to shave. Perhaps he'd grow a beard. Why not? It would be appropriate to a mission everyone at home considered idiotic, irresponsible: to walk out of the bookshop in Bedford Row and make his way to Jerusalem in search of a man no one had heard of, 300 years dead.

If only they knew. What it had meant to be possessed so strangely in the middle of his life, against all sense. If he could, he would have made himself *makeless*, innocent of all earthly goods and ties. As empty-handed as a child he would have come here, barefoot, in penitence and longing.

Thomas looked at his dark reflection in the small mirror and saw the shadow of a man, a fool's face.

He wouldn't sleep yet, he knew. Instead, he took out the leather-bound volume: *William Curthose, his Painefull Peregrination to Jerusalem*.

Thomas read, and as he read, smiled. Poor William, an odd kind of pilgrim. A seventeenth-century sceptic, irritated by monkish guides, mistrustful of Turks, tormented by boils and bowels. A Protestant doubter who, after many trials, fell into faith.

Thomas flicked to the passage immediately following William's: 'bowing of my head at last to my trewe Lord.'

Ah, there it was:

Or, let it be said, this was not so much a bowing, even though I fell upon my knees to kiss the earth, as a Suffusion of my whole Spirit.

Had I been fevered still, as at Aleppo, I would have taken this for *delirium*. For one who has loved much,

23

knowing Women of all sorts, I am taken in Recollection by both the Semblance and the Difference between these two loves, carnal and divine. That is, I fell as we do when our poor, Earthly frames are seized by fleshly Passion, that we mistake our brief spasms for Intimations of Eternitie.

Yet in this failing, I did rise.

Fool's errand, Thomas thought, putting aside the book, lying down. As Teddy never tired of telling him, William could have been as phoney as Mandeville, a pincher and stealer of other men's travellers' tales.

Thomas drifted off to sleep. Something woke him an hour later. It sounded like gunfire or an explosion. Probably a car back-firing.

The candle had guttered low. He snuffed it out.

When Fedor got back Madame Muna was sitting up in bed, her long white hair loosed from its pins. Her hair had always been white, she told Fedor, she had been born with it that colour: a phenomenon her mother had regarded as a mark of special good fortune, once she had got over the shock.

A nest of silk cushions supported her back. She wore her reading glasses and, over her sensible, high-necked night-gown, a home-knitted purple bed-jacket threaded through with blue lurex ribbon. Madame Muna was a legendary knitter and in winter she would have been wearing a bonnet to match, along with her football scarf.

'I was intended,' she would tell Fedor, 'to be a Cubist. My family had hopes for me. Then one day my nurse left her knitting out, I found it and, without any instructions, my fingers flew. I would have been an idiot to go against my destiny.'

'Yes, my darling,' Fedor would say, though the truth was, he was torn. He greatly admired Madame Muna's mastery of stitches, as mysterious as the complexities of the chess board. On the other hand, he dreaded winter – in Jerusalem often quite nippy – and the permanent neck-rash sustained from the wearing of polo-necked collars.

She was knitting now. Fedor had to wait until she had finished a row, then she gave a sigh of satisfaction and patted the bed beside her: the signal for Fedor to put on his pyjamas.

'And how was Magdalena tonight?'

Fedor was used to this question yet it always caught him off guard. He tried to see Eugenia Muna's one vulnerability as endearing.

'I believe she was about. She was busy with a customer.' Fedor made a great business of pulling on his pyjama trousers, to hide the colour of his cheeks. He wondered if he came from a family of blushers.

'Such a beautiful girl.' Madame Muna sighed. 'And she has a good business. It seems a pity that she finds it necessary to sell her assets.'

From long experience Fedor knew how to divert her.

'Unlike you, my dear, she lacks the benefit of background.'

As he settled in bed beside her, Madame Muna patted Fedor's hand.

'That is true. Have I ever told you, I am of a Genoese family descended from one of the last of the children's crusades? The German boy, Nicholas, who set out not to kill but to convert the Moslems. I believe it is understood in Genoa to be a mark of distinction. A number of the wretched children got no further than Genoa, you see, and the lucky ones were adopted and allowed to stay.'

She put down her knitting, took off her spectacles and settled more comfortably against the cushions.

'You know, Fedor, I am sometimes very tired. I am not a woman who speaks much of her feelings but my feet are so cold lately. If you ever left me I should be old.'

'I would never leave you, Eugenia. I could not live without you.'

'My dear Fedor.'

They sat side by side, comfortably, as they had for longer than either could remember. The ritual was always the same. First, Eugenia passed Fedor the silver-backed brush from her side of the bed and he brushed her beautiful hair for a hundred strokes. As he brushed, she closed her eyes and smiled and became a child again, sitting as a favourite maid brushed her hair in the nursery on the Golden Horn.

When Fedor had finished brushing, he kissed first Eugenia's

hands, then her lips, and sometimes, if they were available, her feet.

Then it was his turn. With the gentleness of a mother and the pleasure of a mistress (even though, apparently, they had never made love), she took his face in her hands, kissed him and brought his head to her breast. There he rested in a state of bliss (he told himself) that surely transcended all carnal love he had known. When Eugenia made to sleep, he whispered, as he often did, the same question.

'When will we make love, my darling?'

And Eugenia gave the familiar answer.

'One day, Fedor, one day.'

Sinking back against his own pillows, Fedor pondered that promise of 'one day'. He told himself sternly that even without fleshly love, with its sweating and its sighing, he would never come to the end of Eugenia. She was a boundless country, a continent. He loved her for her scent of hyacinths and the sweetness of her hair, but also, nowadays, for her frailties.

He listened to her purring snore and wondered if he were perverted to be so transported by cold feet and bunions and no sex when musky Magdalena was almost certainly available at a reduced fee, possibly gratis.

Maybe Eugenia was right to be jealous. Fedor was tempted. Only a passion as binding and ever-forgiving as his would ever have persuaded him to accept the arrangement Eugenia had laid down all those years ago.

Perhaps it was the weather or the rumble of history outside, or this evening's sniff of musky Magdalena. Whatever the cause, Fedor was seized tonight by a small rebellion against Eugenia's promise. Jerusalem had fallen so often. The next time could be the last. Then 'one day' would be too late.

Restless, he got up and still in his nightshirt went down to the cool garden to smoke one of his thin black cigars. The moon-flowers had opened their faces to gaze at their mistress in the sky. There was the rustle of a cat disturbed.

Fedor knew, as suddenly and certainly as though the banyan tree had spoken, that were he to lie in Magdalena's bed, he would be forever exiled from Eugenia's arms. Even though she might know nothing of his infidelity, some magic would banish him.

Love, he thought. How many hundred thousand times I have told her I love her. And why, never once, has she spoken? Why will she not permit consummation? And why did it matter, when Eugenia had been sister, companion, flower-garden, jungle? Jittering cry of monkeys, soft blue flight of birds; ocean, desert, sunrise, sunset; the quiet of milk in a glass, the yell of fireworks, trumpets; red of passion, purple anger. For her rage was royal.

Absently, Fedor ground out his cigar with his heel and was about to throw the butt into the flower-bed when someone spoke at his shoulder.

'Oh, please not in the moon-flowers.'

'Miss Mary.'

'I hope I didn't startle you. I couldn't sleep, you see. So I thought a walk in the garden.'

Fedor had always liked their only permanent lodger. She struck him as a shrewd woman, a little sad perhaps, but there was a calmness about her that made her company as welcome sometimes as a rest in the shade after Eugenia's sun.

Very little was known about her. She looked semitic and yet she was a Christian (but then there had been an Arch-deacon of Jerusalem who was a Palestinian Israeli citizen). She was said to have spent the war in Egypt and to have lived once in Jericho. She rarely left Israel, except for her annual trip to Cairo. Much of the time, with her small cat at her heels, she spent cultivating the garden and even now she was smiling at her precious moon-flowers.

'Isn't the scent wonderful? It only blooms at night, you know. *Ipomaea Bonanox* – known for its fragrance and large white flowers. Tropical. It's amazing it survives here.'

'You are an amazing gardener, Miss Mary.'

'Thank you, Fedor. Shall we sit down? I do like the sound of the water at night. You and I did a good job there.'

Fedor remembered. What had appeared to be nothing more than a useless stream ('drains,' Eugenia had said), at times of heavy rain flooding the small garden, had turned out to be a spring from what had once been bare hillside. Miss Mary had found it and together she and Fedor had worked. Under her direction he had built the retaining wall and set in concrete the stone lion's head from whose mouth the stream now gushed, tumbling as a waterfall into a fish-pool.

'Why don't you have another of your cigars, Fedor?'

'If you don't mind?'

'Of course not. Is there something on your mind, Fedor? Anything you would like to talk about?'

Sometimes Fedor wondered if Miss Mary was psychic. Then he thought it was more likely that she had been a school-teacher. Either way, she had eyes in the back of her brain. She could see not only what you were doing behind her back but what you were thinking.

Fedor took out a cigar and dug in his pocket for matches.

'To tell you the truth I was thinking about love. In a general way, of course,' he added hastily. One did not discuss Eugenia at a stone's throw from her bedroom window. Even sleeping, she had ears that went round corners.

'I mean, it's a word we use all the time but what is it?' Fedor felt shy, even with Miss Mary, of speaking out in such a way. His role was normally that of a listener. Eugenia had long ago allotted him this posture. And with Solly and Hamil his major utterances were those of the story-teller. Between them, the other two talked enough for a school of Talmud scholars.

'If only we could define it in the concrete,' Feodor went on wistfully. 'Colour, for instance.'

Miss Mary always thought before she replied. That was another thing about her that Fedor liked.

'I'd say all the colours in the range from violet through rose and gold to red. And I have sometimes imagined it to be a little like the Holy Ghost. Less blue, though.'

Fedor nodded. He did not like to say that he had as much difficulty with the Holy Ghost. More, even. This was, he suspected, something to do with his lost childhood, from which there surfaced now and then a sound, a scent, the warmth of a lap; the smell of wash-day; the picture of a ripe plum and the feel of a wasp's sting; a child's cry (his own?) and a strong, rough, woman's hand, sound of women's voices, just beyond the range of understanding. Ordinary things. And then the wasp frightened him and opened the door on something alarming he did not like: a procession, candled darkness, and while everyone sang a child saw the Ghost himself in the shape of coiled shadows in a corner.

He could never go further than that, nor did he wish to. But every time he smelled incense, he felt sick.

Then the sky cracked as it so often did these nights in Jerusalem. Fedor stood. He felt as small as when the first picture of earth came back from space. Frantic worms, Solly said we were, occupying no more than a brief blink in time. Such a fuss, such wringing of hands. So many questions and no time for answers before we're put out.

But Solly could laugh about that. He had his faith.

Fedor knew there was little point in covering your head, not in this place, there was no cover.

'Do you think we'll ever have peace?'

Miss Mary had moved as sometimes she did, so soundlessly you found yourself talking to an empty seat, and there she was at your shoulder, dead-heading the roses.

'Oh yes,' she said, brushing the soil from her hands. 'Not yet. But there will be peace.'

FOUR

There was something about Madame Muna's: something, it was conjectured, in the water perhaps, or the wine. Or even in time, as though somehow continuity had fallen over itself, been wrinkled by a playful thumb. So that there were those who came and went in an ordinary way, taking home nothing more interesting than indigestion from an excess of Carmel with dubious goat. And those who had intimations or dreams and would claim wildly or soberly according to their natures, that they had seen through the fantasy of history and of time, and witnessed Tolstoy and Henry Kissinger dining rowdily together, then joining arm in arm to dance and sing a chorus of *Fiddler on the Roof.*

In another historical wrinkle, Freud went not to London to die but gave Anna and Martha the slip and came here to Eugenia's small garden. He threw away his prosthesis, lived on honey and yoghurt and declared himself a Jungian. He died in a spasm of extreme bliss.

As Eugenia Muna always said: 'History is not a train but water in a bucket. Slosh it around and anything might slop over. Everything is there – the beginning and the middle and the end.'

She also said: 'There is nothing that has happened that will not happen again. Until everything is finished.'

'And what will the end be, Eugenia?' Fedor would ask.

'Sufficient unto the day,' Madame Muna would say and pick up her dropped stitches.

Fedor would nod thankfully. He had enough on his plate, what with love and forgetfulness and his soft spot for Magdalena, not to mention the Holy Ghost.

★

Eugenia lingered in bed, sipping her jasmine tea. The truth was that she did not tell Fedor what the end would be because she did not know. Aware though she was of the peculiar quality of time in her guest-house, she accepted this as one does the weather.

She sensed that dear Fedor chose to see her as prescient and if he enjoyed the concept she was happy enough to sustain it. Privately though, she was grateful not to know when and if Jerusalem would fall again. It was, after all, the only true home she had ever acknowledged.

'Home is where the heart is,' Fedor would say. Eugenia was not quite sure about that, since she was by no means certain that she had a heart. Lately, there had been flutterings but that could have been cheese.

Eugenia shook her head as she listened to the morning news. Yesterday's Crusaders, today's Americans, oil or God, it all came to the same thing and it was always Jerusalem that bore the brunt in the end.

She had dreamed of this, or possibly heard it and forgotten where: Hep, Hep! That terrible bark. *Hierosolayme est perdita!*

Eugenia set down her cup and put in her teeth. It was a pointless gesture but gestures mattered. So she made a note on the pad by the bed. RE GAS MASKS REMIND FEDOR.

Daisy woke to an intense orgasm, in fact, the first orgasm she had ever had. She never knew that it had been sparked by a ripple from an earthquake in Mesopotamia: six on the Richter scale, quite shattering in the Garden of Eden.

When she sat up she found she was blushing and still suffused with an altogether delightful warmth.

She knew what had happened to her. She had read about it in magazines at the hairdresser's, a little wistfully, for her sexual experiences to date had yielded nothing more interesting than a tickle in the nose climaxing in a sneeze. An allergy, she had supposed.

What a pity there had been no one to share it with. Regretfully, she took a cold shower.

★

31

'Tell me, is there a nun here?'

Daisy asked her question as Fedor was pouring her coffee into the big breakfast cup. Mornings were not his best time and he had been startled to find the English woman already sitting at a table out of doors when he came down at seven o'clock.

The way that Israel seemed to bounce out of bed with hardly a blink or a yawn was a custom to which he had never attuned himself. He came out to serve Daisy still in his slippers, unshaven, with his pyjama jacket pushed inside his trousers. His hand shook slightly and the coffee-pot clinked against the cup. At least it was one mercy that Eugenia refused to serve the famous Israeli breakfast.

'There will be nuns,' Fedor said. 'But there are not nuns yet.'

'But I saw one. Last night,' Daisy said. 'Something woke me up, a noise like a bang. I looked out of the window to see if there was a thunderstorm and you were in the garden with a woman in a wimple.'

'A wimple? Ah yes, that must have been Miss Mary, our lodger. It is not really a wimple. That is to say, she is not a nun, but she chooses to wear it.'

'I see,' Daisy said, although she did not see at all.

She was about to go back to her coffee and her guide-book when at the same moment someone knocked into the chair on her right, ducked to pick it up, dropped some papers, dived to collect them together and at last stood up. Or rather, not quite up but with his neck a little bent as if he expected to hit his head even under the sky, even out of doors.

'Sorry. I'm really terribly sorry. Good morning.'

'Good morning.' The man from the plane. 'No harm done. Really.' Daisy wondered if he was growing a beard or had forgotten to shave. 'I saw you on the plane. My name's Daisy Herbert.'

'Thomas Curtis. My favourite poet.'

'Who?'

'George Herbert.'

'Oh yes. Did you say Curtis?'

32

'Yes. Probably from the old French. A Crusader name,' he offered tentatively. 'Curthose. Short stockings, I suppose.'

'Yes, I expect so.' Daisy was getting a crick in her neck. 'Won't you sit down?'

'That's frightfully kind.'

Daisy watched apprehensively as Thomas folded himself into the small iron chair. M. Hulot sits down.

'I'm trying to shake off a cousin,' she said. 'What are you doing in Jerusalem?'

'A cousin?'

'Barbara. You know, a bit like Charlotte in *A Room with a View*. That is, she tries to stop people enjoying themselves. We were with a package then everyone cancelled because of the crisis, except me. I didn't tell Barbara I was coming until half an hour before I left. She disapproves dreadfully but she's determined to follow. But I shouldn't talk about her like that. She means well.' Daisy smiled. 'That's an awful thing to say about anyone, isn't it? But you were saying, why you're here?'

Thomas looked at the young woman with the burning bush of red hair. He had come to Jerusalem with one purpose. In the spirit of his passionate pilgrimage there was no room for girls with extraordinary hair and smiling eyes and a nice mouth.

'Please forgive me. I've just remembered. An appointment. I say, I *am* sorry!'

It was just as well that Fedor was nippy on his feet from his tea-dance days or Thomas would have sent him flying along with tray, cup and coffee-pot.

Daisy and Fedor watched him flail his way indoors, forgetting to duck. He appeared to be apologising to the door for banging his head.

'Do tell me your name.'

'Fedor.'

'You're not Israeli, are you? Or Arab?'

Fedor shook his head.

'Well,' Daisy said, 'I suppose I'd better get started. I'm booked on a tour this morning. Fedor, will you do me a favour?'

'Of course.'

'If a Miss Banks, Barbara Banks, asks for me, you've never seen me. I'm not here.'

'Never in the whole of my life have I seen you.'

'Bless you, Fedor.'

As she turned away, a movement in the lower garden caught Daisy's eye.

'Oh, look, there's that nun who isn't a nun. With that extraordinary-looking woman. I wonder what they're doing. They seem to be measuring something. Oh well, I'd better run.'

'Fedor.'

'Eugenia. Miss Mary.'

Fedor trotted down the steps from the terrace to join the two women. He mopped his brow. It was unusually hot for Succot, even so early in the day. Eugenia had abandoned both her sheepskin boots and her football scarf. She wore one of her triangular kaftans, with her abundant hair piled inside a wide-brimmed straw hat. Miss Mary had settled for a cotton version of the sensible blue flying-suit she favoured for gardening.

'Fedor,' Eugenia said, 'my feet are too big, Miss Mary's are too small. Yours are exactly one foot, I know. Please pace out six feet by six in the flower-bed, here. Then you can mark it with pegs and string and start digging.'

'Digging?'

When Daisy refused to cancel, Barbara had pulled her lemon face and pressed on her the address and telephone number of Morgan Pooley, curate to the Anglican Church in Jerusalem. She said something about him writing a book. This was the sort of contact Barbara made a special point of collecting from all over the world. It went with her hot-line to God, whom, Daisy felt sure, Barbara saw as a white Anglo-Saxon Protestant Santa Claus sitting on a comfortable cloud in a blaze of glory writing down people's names, with Barbara's at the top. Once, Daisy remarked that the Old Testament God struck her as midway between the deceased Ayatollah

Khomeni and Saddam Hussein. She had been hoping to provoke her cousin but Barbara was not offended. Along with the Crusaders, she was invincibly New Testament. At primary school she had won the Christmas competition for the neatest crib.

Daisy could imagine vividly what Morgan Pooley would be like: thin, with cold hands and one of those churchy voices. She supposed she would have to see him. There had been a note in her pigeon-hole this morning after breakfast: 'I should be very glad if you would care to join us at six o'clock this evening. Morgan Pooley.' There was a small map enclosed, showing the Damascus Gate and a street called Derech Sechem. Also the bus station and the house, apartment, or whatever it was, where the Reverend Pooley was to be found, near St George's Cathedral.

Bother Barbara. She must have written the very day Daisy announced her intention to carry on with the trip.

Climbing into the minibus where the big coaches waited outside the Jaffa Gate, Daisy resolved to put her cousin and everything to do with her out of her mind. She had come to see Jerusalem and see it she would.

The first thing Daisy noticed was that everything was much smaller than she had expected. The second, that their guide was rather dishy.

'My name is Gideon,' the young man said. 'Here we are in Bethany where Jesus Christ visited often with Lazarus and his sisters, Mary and Martha. As you see, it is still a village. From here we proceed to the Mount of Olives. You have ten minutes now to take photographs.'

Daisy did not like being told what to see and how to see it. She did not care for guided tours and was already rebelling against this one as she left the Franciscan Sanctuary of Lazarus and made her way not down, where everyone had their video-cameras whirring, but up to the ruined tower above. From here she shaded her eyes to look across desert and scrub.

'I'd no idea the desert was so close,' she said. Gideon looked like a warrior, she decided. A shade too stern to be really dishy. Unlike the Arab thwacking a bow-legged donkey up the road below, he did not seem part of the landscape. 'It's beautiful.'

Gideon frowned at the desert.

'You must visit the Peace Forest,' he said. 'We have an afforestation programme second to none in the world.'

Barbara would like that, Daisy thought. She would want to know how many trees and write the figure down. Which reminded Daisy that she was supposed to be making notes to give or send to Barbara. The trouble was, she and Barbara were not looking for the same things. Barbara would know all about Barluzzi, who designed the sanctuary. She would tidy everything up for future reference, while Daisy would remember Bethany for gorgeous Gideon's frown, the desert, and the Arab who had now stopped beating his donkey and was sitting under a eucalyptus tree hawking up some good phlegm.

'Are you a soldier?' Daisy asked Gideon, as she gazed out in the direction of Jericho and the Dead Sea.

'Everyone in Israel is a soldier.'

'Oh. Sorry. Of course.'

Daisy wondered where in all this was Christ? If he had ever been, this was perhaps the last place to look for him. Too many footsteps, too much blood, oceans of blood.

Certainly not in the weird Crusader Church of Mary's tomb, more like a souk than a church, where Daisy wondered what Barbara would make of the incense-holders hung with Christmas balls, and herself felt dizzy: there was a darkness at the end. She thought of bats and almost wished Barbara was there, to cut the shadows down to size with sensible Anglican scissors.

And yet there was something? It was the heat probably or expectation or Gideon's sublime profile, but in the Garden of Gethsemane Daisy felt that there was a sad, tired, longing presence.

Gideon was explaining to the small party, with an air of faint disapproval, that Christ had spent his last night here before going into Jerusalem, because no Jew on that day of the week would go beyond the Sabbat stones, when Daisy's back prickled.

'Below is the Golden Gate,' Gideon said. 'Here the Messiah will arrive and for this reason the heroes of Zion are buried, that they may be first among the many.'

But she was listening and not listening. This was the vision she had held in her head, behind her eyes. There was the golden Mosque of Omar, and the El-Aqsa Mosque, where the Temple had stood, the wall around Jerusalem. Yet she turned away towards the garden and the olive trees, thick-boled with time, thinking, absurdly, she might catch him, not weeping for Jerusalem, not about to die, but moving among the trees, by the olive-press.

She caught her breath. There in her dazzled eyes was a blue shape, a rag of a man, going away.

Of course, not Christ, who would hardly come down from heaven after nearly two thousand years, to show himself to Daisy Herbert. There was no mistaking the flamingo gait, the anxiously folded shoulders: Thomas Short-stockings giving Daisy a half-wave as he left the Garden of Gethsemane, all by himself, alone.

A voice at her shoulder made Daisy jump.

'You are at Madame Muna's,' said gorgeous Gideon. 'I shall call on you there.'

Eugenia drank lemonade spliced with vodka while Fedor dug.

'No, Fedor,' Eugenia called, from under the shade of the banyan tree, 'a little to the left.'

Fedor stuck the spade into the earth and mopped his brow.

'It won't work, Eugenia. It's not nearly big enough for an air-raid shelter.'

'Of course it isn't. But underneath the foundations there is a cave. The entrance has been blocked by earth for three hundred years. It won't do any good, I fear, but our guests will expect a shelter. When you have finished that you can fetch the gas-masks.'

While Fedor dug, Eugenia's mind was on other matters. Preparing for the end was a job that had to be done but not one she relished. She felt herself to be at once afloat in time and anchored here. Her predicament was one probably shared by many. What marked her out was that she not only knew time to be a loop but could bear witness to the fact. If she half-closed her eyes the present would dissolve in the shaking light and there would be David in his old age: cold with his years, finding comfort without consummation in the arms of Abishag, his shallow sleep troubled by the dash of a jet-fighter cracking the high air.

Time to come and time past. Her own linear history so strangely tangled with this eternal damnfool city: its kings and occupiers and pilgrims and lovers.

Lovers. That reminded Eugenia. She had laid plans for the girl Daisy and the man Thomas. She had intended them to be struck by love at their first breakfast here, this morning. If she had been writing a novel that is what would have happened. But her omnipotence was not authorial and her omniscience patchy. Anything could have turned the head of an impressionable female seeing Jerusalem for the first time, unchaperoned.

Ah! There was the sound of a minibus pulling up, doors slamming, voices, footsteps.

Eugenia opened her eyes and closed them again at once.

The Little Sisters of Sorrow had arrived. Bloody nuns.

A long way from Jerusalem two travellers unknown to one another, were about to share a table in the Heathrow Penta coffee-shop.

'Excuse me,' Teddy Short said. 'Is this place taken?'

'Help yourself.' Barbara Banks, managing editor of Hay & Windo, was tucking into a steak.

Teddy Short, of the Antiquarian Bookshop in Bedford Row, took his seat and glumly surveyed the menu. He already had nervous indigestion and the prevailing smell of curry did not help. Nor did the plain woman on the other side of the table, though at least she was English and that must be something.

It is thanks to Thomas, Teddy thought, chewing something bloody, that I am stuck in this impossible place, waiting to fly, which is what I most hate doing in this world, and unable to take off.

38

The worst of every world. Flying. Thomas gone off his head with some fantasy about pilgrimage to an area that was certainly about to become a war zone. And only batty Betty left to mind the shop.

Then almost all flights over most of the planet suspended. In particular, El Al was wilfully giving out no information about when if ever it might next take off for Tel Aviv.

Standby felt to Teddy, hideously permanent. As in forever.

FIVE

'So what do you think of Jerusalem?'

'Oh Lord, I don't know.' In Morgan Pooley's flat Daisy looked round hopefully for the tray of nibbles. All day she had not wanted to eat and now she was starving. And beginning to get weary of the same question. 'I mean, there are so many Jerusalems. It depends which, doesn't it? Of course, it's wonderful.'

Thomas Short-stockings was doing a dangerous balancing act with a glass and a sausage on a stick. Daisy decided he was definitely growing a beard. He appeared as tired as she felt. She had a second's absurd urge to put her arms around him, rest his head on her shoulder and pat him on the back. But Eugenia's perception of Daisy as a naïve child was entirely wrong. She was not a child but a woman who could quite well take care of herself (as she had told Barbara and as Barbara refused to appreciate).

So instead of embracing Thomas, she said: 'How are you getting around? I saw you in the Garden of Gethsemane this morning.'

'Did you? How astonishing.'

'Not really. Jerusalem's a small place. Very confusing though. I tried to find the Holy Sepulchre this afternoon but the Old City's more like a souk. Maybe that's the best way to find Jerusalem – to lose yourself. Have you got a guide?'

'Not exactly. I've read some of the old pilgrims. Wey and a few others. I've even looked at Sweyn and Saewulf. But it's a post-Reformation chap I'm interested in. Rather unusual in those days. He had some kind of vision. Actually, he's a sort of ancestor. The one I mentioned.'

'How exciting.'

'It might be if I knew where to start. Everything looked different then. There wasn't so much of it, apart from anything else. They had a frightful time. Mamelukes and Saracens. You know.'

Daisy didn't know but she smiled and was about to ask when their host intervened. Morgan Pooley was pleased with the way his party was going and especially delighted with Daisy, who had turned out, with her amazing hair, appealing expression and general friendliness, to be as unlike her dreaded cousin as it was possible to imagine.

'And what are you two talking about?'

With the air of a windy heron, Thomas dipped his head and ducked away. Daisy looked at Morgan Pooley. He was a bit thin and a shade too smooth round the chin but his hand when she shook it had been dry and he didn't seem at all preachy. Quite cosy, in fact.

'Pilgrims,' she said.

Morgan sketched a sigh with his hand.

'Oh dear, yes, this time of year. Succot and all that. At least this year we'll be spared most of the foreign tours, what with the new mad mahdi out there. Jesus Tours are bringing some Anglican nuns, otherwise the Garden Tomb's more or less closed while the archeologists do their thing. Ever since they found the fish.'

'The fish?'

'The fish. You know. But you'll come, I hope. If I say it myself, it's a lovely garden.' Pooley waved to someone approaching: an elderly man, stout, with pebble spectacles. The party had thickened and reached shouting level. Morgan put his paw on Daisy's wrist. 'You will be careful, won't you. Things are a bit dodgy. You'll be OK at Madame Muna's but don't wander around by yourself, especially in the Old City. Now we've found you we don't want to lose you. Solly – come and tell our new friend not to hike around alone. Daisy, this is Solomon Herzog. Rabbi. Daisy's at Madame Muna's. Must dash. Now, you promise, you'll come and see us? The Garden and the Tomb, I mean?'

'Yes. I will. Thank you.'

41

Daisy was beginning to feel dizzy. The rabbi was beaming.

'Shall we sit down?'

'Yes, let's.' Daisy's tone was grateful.

'And tell me, are you by any chance hungry?'

'Absolutely ravenous.'

'Now,' Solomon said, having delivered a loaded plate and settled them both in a window-seat. 'Tell me what you think of Jerusalem.'

'Well, I've only been here a day.'

'And everyone has asked you the same question.'

'Yes, actually, they have.'

'That is because, for us, it is a special place.'

Daisy wondered if she was in for a lecture but it seemed not. She scanned the party. Vaguely, she was keeping an eye open for Thomas. He struck her as someone in need of care and protection. She also rather liked that hollow at the base of his throat revealed by his open-necked shirt. No point in dwelling on that though. His gaze, she suspected, was fixed elsewhere.

'To tell you the truth, I am in rather a muddle. There's all the old stuff. I don't know whether to read the Old Testament or the New Testament or Runciman or what. I mean, my head's full of bits from the Bible. Then I come here and everyone's talking about war, and I'm warned not to travel. I'm supposed to like those churches that have been dumped over everything that wasn't already covered up. But I think that Italian architect Barluzzi is boring. People keep talking *at* me. The whole place is like someone with a temperature. I don't know what I'm looking for but whatever it is, I can't find it. And yet everyone's right. It *is* wonderful.'

With horror, Daisy heard herself going on. To her surprise the rabbi's expression was still genial. She caught snatches of conversation. A very English home-counties voice was complaining that it was really all too much, one couldn't even be sure of Earl Grey any more. And someone less petulant but still English was asking wistfully if the annual picnic in the Peace Forest was still on. Morgan Pooley

42

appeared to have been de-bounced by a large woman in pearls and Pringle twin-set who looked about to crush his skull.

'Oh, I am so sorry,' Daisy said. 'I never talk like that usually. Please forgive me. Too much in one day, I suppose. What do you think I should read?'

'Nothing or everything.' Daisy had a feeling that in the mildest way, she was being teased, but she didn't mind. Solomon went on: 'The Psalms maybe. Look for the stars. He telleth the number of the stars; he calleth them all by their names. The Koran if you have time.'

'The Koran?'

'You might be surprised. There was a time when you and I were the People of the Book, deserving protection and respect. Friends of Islam, if misguided. Well, now we have the intifada and twenty-nine political parties fighting for the Knesset. Politics. Best of all, look. I hope you will.' Solomon laughed. Some private joke. 'This is a crazy city, a mad country. But, you know, it is the only place in the world I feel at home. The new generation, like my grandson Gideon, I am not sure what they make of it. Gideon, for instance, has the anger but I am not certain he has the love. Who can blame him? He lost his father in the Yom Kippur war. His is a very ordinary story.'

Daisy looked at Solomon. She was fascinated by the way he talked with his hands. And she felt a little shy. A naïve Englishwoman who might do better not to open her mouth. Curiosity compelled her, though. It usually did.

'Don't you find the present situation terrifying?'

'It has happened before. It will happen again. Each time they move the goal-posts. Besides, I am much too old to run for cover any more.'

'It seems a frightful mess.'

'Indeed.' Solomon nodded several times. The silence was prolonged and Daisy wondered if the rabbi might have dropped off. Morgan Pooley's lighting was dim. Candles were guttering, the power flickered. Then Solomon snapped wide awake. His white tuft of hair stood up on his otherwise bald pate. 'But it is still the most blessed miracle, this land.

43

The Land. You will see. Succot. How the pilgrims come. Meanwhile there is always chess. Do you play chess?'

'I'm afraid not.'

'What a pity. But you are at Madame Muna's so you know my good friend Fedor.'

'Fedor? Oh yes. He's sweet. Do you play chess with him?'

'Not exactly. That is, he has other gifts.' Solomon stood. 'That reminds me, I was to meet him tonight. I am late.'

'Is it all right to walk around at night?'

The Israeli shrug; Daisy was becoming quite familiar with this way of saying, who cares, I go my own way.

'The greatest pleasure to meet you, my dear. Take care. You will find Jerusalem is, of all places, anything you wish it to be.' Solomon smiled. He shook her hand. 'Goodnight.'

'Before you go, tell me, what is Succot?'

'The end of the reading of the Torah. And the Feast of the Tabernacles. A harvest festival in a sense. You see, there is nothing new under the sun. Everything is different. But if you step just a little further back, everything is the same.'

'So you'll come to the picnic?' Morgan said. 'It is rather jolly. Do come.'

Daisy had to admit that there was something persuasive about Morgan Pooley. Intending to commit herself to nothing, she had apparently agreed to visit the Garden Tomb and now could find no reason not to accept this second invitation. He had caught her just as she was about to leave.

'Picnic?'

'The annual Anglican picnic in the Peace Forest. It's more fun than it sounds. No prayers. But I have to admit, rather a shortage of stunning young women. So you will come?'

'Well, I suppose.'

If he were a dog, Daisy thought, he would be wagging his tail in a keen kind of way. She sometimes thought of people as dogs. For instance, Thomas Short-stockings who had reappeared from nowhere, it seemed, and was now waiting for them to walk back to Madame Muna's together, would be something rangy like an Irish Wolfhound with a mix of some less well-coordinated breed.

44

She had a feeling that if she didn't go now Thomas would disappear again. And she had been a little abrupt with Morgan.

'Yes, thank you, I'd like that very much. And thank you for a lovely party.'

Bother. Thomas had vanished, Daisy had refused a taxi and now she would have to catch him up.

For a moment she stood confused in the narrow street. From what she could remember of the map it would be quicker to go through the Damascus Gate, more prudent to take the road outside the walls.

Just as she had decided definitely to stick to the main road and look out for a taxi, those peculiar shadows under the overhanging fig moved and made Daisy jump.

'Sorry,' Thomas said. 'Don't much care for parties.'

'I don't either,' Daisy said. 'People are never themselves, are they?'

It was difficult to keep up with Thomas. He loped. She trotted, very nearly had to run. He seemed to have taken a vow not to look at her, which made conversation doubly difficult. It was hard enough already, watching out for slippery steps and sudden corners as they made their way through the darkened city of shutters and closed and bolted doors and smells both revolting and delicious: drains and spice. As for Solomon's stars, there was not a glimpse to be had of them.

Thomas strode on, attempting to put behind him all girls with flaming hair, the present political situation, the thought of Teddy possibly in pursuit, certainly upset.

'Have you read Raleigh?' he said.

Daisy was too out of breath to answer, so he told her. '"Give me my scallop shell of quiet, My Staffe of Faith to walk upon, My scrip of joy, Immortal diet, My bottle of salvation: My gowne of glory, hopes true gage And thus I'll take my pilgrimage."'

'About to die, he wrote that, of death.'

'It's wonderful,' she said, at last, when they paused in a small square, with a high wall and a gate leading off. Here she could see the moon and the stars. Thomas's uplifted face was

45

beautiful, beyond normal knowing, for those few moments. 'But love's better. Love can redeem everything, can't it. Love divine.'

'Divine love, yes. Actually, I'm thinking of becoming a monk.'

While Daisy and Thomas were making their way back through the Old City, too busy watching the stars to realise that they themselves were being watched, Hamil, Solomon and Fedor were, at Hamil's request, holding an extraordinary general meeting at Magdalena's. Because of the night chill they were not in the garden but occupied a table in the corner of the empty bar.

Business was bad, Magdalena said, wiping the zinc bar-top and rearranging the dusty plastic flowers. With things as they were, people were not so keen to go out at night, even by the secret way to Magdalena's.

'The poor men,' she said. 'They are having to make love to their wives.'

In fact, Fedor was wondering how Solly moved around so freely. It was generally considered imprudent for a Jew to wander the Old City at night. Many were avoiding it even by day. Did his friend the rabbi move in a cloak of invisibility? Under Eugenia Muna's tuition Fedor had learned long ago that nothing, in or out of this world, was impossible.

Fedor arrived last, out of breath. It had been difficult getting away from Eugenia.

'No chess?'

'No chess tonight,' Solly said.

'I'm afraid I have no story.'

'No stories either.' Solly looked unusually serious. 'Hamil has something to tell us.'

The imam cleared his throat. He looked around, as he always did before he spoke, a habit that made Fedor nervous, even though he had never seen anything dangerous at Hamil's shoulder.

'Tonight we break our rule,' he said. 'Though what I have to say has to do not so much with politics or religion as with prophecy.' He lowered his head and so did the other two, even though there was no one but the mynah bird on the bar to hear them. Magdalena had gone upstairs. 'You know in the hadith it is foretold that before the Day of Judgement and the opening of the graves, there will come the imposter-Messiah, the enemy of Allah, and for a time he will rule. He shall be recognised by a sign: the one eye.'

Fedor did not know any of this but he nodded while Hamil Ibn Abbas Sartawi paused for effect.

The imam went on: 'I believe he is come. He was among us all the time. Have you not noticed? The filthy social diseases of Kalfayan the Armenian have reached one of his eyes. He wears a patch but it is said that the socket is hollow. He opened his eye one morning and it fell into his yoghurt. That piece of dirt! Dung is too good a word for him. Dung is without spite. It is useful.'

Fedor's mouth was open. It was Solly who spoke.

'You could be right, my dear fellow, but what can we do about it?'

Hamil spat neatly, a precise, remarkably rounded gob. Happily it landed on the floor, not the table. Spitting appeared to be an atavistic desert habit he had not quite shaken off.

'It is written that Isa will descend to earth in armour to kill him.'

'Armour?' said Fedor.

Hamil waved his hand in a slicing motion.

'A fighter plane it could be. Or a tank of your friends the Americans.'

Hamil looked as though he might be about to spit again.

'Oh, I do hope not,' Fedor said. He didn't care for wars and had never become accustomed to living in a part of the world where war or threat of war was on the daily agenda. 'Is there no way round it?'

'It might be acceptable to Allah if we were to destroy him ourselves.'

There was a long silence, even from the loquacious Solly, while everyone wondered how.

Fedor spoke in a small voice.

'Who's Isa, anyway?'

'Your Jesus,' said Hamil.

47

That was very interesting, Fedor thought. Or it would have been if the imam hadn't got him so worried.

'I think,' he offered, 'that we should all have a drink.'

So they did. Solly called Magdalena and she brought coffee for Hamil, angels' pee for Solly and Fedor.

It was Solly who said what Fedor was thinking.

'Let us sleep on this. I believe we should take no drastic action. There are troubles enough already.'

Hamil growled. 'Are you impugning Mohammed?'

'Never, my friend. But I consider for the moment we should return to the rules of which we have never spoken. No politics, no religion. Chess and stories. Meanwhile keeping an eye on the Armenian.'

'Keeping an eye!' Fedor laughed. The other two looked at him. Apparently this was not a joke.

Solly stood, heavily.

'And now we must go our ways. In peace, I hope, and love. And Hamil, look not too much for portents. We have quite enough trouble as it is.'

So they shook hands.

'Peace and love,' Solly repeated and Fedor echoed him.

And the mynah bird echoed Fedor: 'Peaceanlove!'

As the three figures, one tall, one broad and one so skinny you could hardly see him sideways, left Magdalena's, in another part of the night city outside the walls, Morgan Pooley lay awake. He thought about his party and the picnic to come and various other matters, and found to his surprise how many considerations seemed to lead to Daisy Herbert. Not exactly in a physical sense but in an unusually cheerful way that put the Song of Songs temporarily out of his head.

He had never really understood what love was but just in the blink before he dropped off Morgan did wonder if he had fallen into something with Daisy. Could it be love? .

Below Morgan's window the gardener no one had ever seen, who worked only at night, pinched a leaf and sniffed again that kindly herb that brings sleep and a little comfort: myrrh.

SIX

At the Heathrow Penta Barbara Banks had taken two showers, and rung the desk to complain that there was no Gideon Bible in the bedside table, the Kleenex dispenser was empty and she required a pot of tea without tea-bags.

She was directed to call housekeeping for the Kleenex dispenser and room-service for the tea.

'I have called them already. They appear unable to comprehend my requests. They do not speak English. Possibly they are Indonesian. This is not to be held against them. I consider that the management should have taken steps to instruct them in English.'

'Tea-making facilities are supplied in every room.'

'Tea-bags, not tea.'

Barbara snorted and put down the telephone. She had always reckoned she was at home anywhere. It was a small and forgivable point of pride, she had remarked more than once to Daisy, that she had travelled by train through Mongolia on high-fibre biscuits and dried figs, camped with a small butane gas-ring in the High Atlas in pouring rain and the Berbers had called her mother.

Here, however, she was not at home. In the streets of Calcutta she could have set up her mental wigwam but an airport hotel had defeated her. She would make herself a cup of tea then go down to the desk to check the latest position on the El Al flight. As things stood, they had been warned not to go home (oh, how she longed for Berkhamsted) as check-in might be announced at any time.

Yes, that was it. A schedule always helped. Tea. Television. Desk. Dinner. Come on Barbara, pull up your socks.

49

So Barbara made her tea and settled down to watch television. She would not blame Daisy, without whose strong-headed folly she would not be here. On whose behalf, in a sense, she was now watching, in bewildered horror, what appeared to be turtles (or tortoises) with green shells talking American and eating pizzas.

On the other side of the corridor in a room that exactly mirrored Barbara's, Teddy Short, wearing the silk dressing-gown he had given himself for his birthday, was glumly eating the smoked salmon sandwiches he had prepared the day before yesterday for the flight. On the few occasions he was obliged to fly, Teddy always avoided aircraft food. He had put the sandwiches in the bedroom fridge which appeared to serve no purpose at all, since it contained nothing. The half bottle of Sancerre he had ordered was not too bad but nor was it cold.

Teddy was not even cheered by a rather delicious nineteenth-century edition of Sir Thomas Browne he had picked up in a house sale and withheld from the bookshelves in Bedford Row. The feel of the pages, the smell, the perfection of the prose, he had brought for his comfort in the same frame of mind in which he had cut the triangular sandwiches. But the trouble with Browne was that, read in the wrong mood, the gentle stoic became a frightful gloomy-boots: all graves and ashes and dreadful warnings.

The best thing to do was to put aside the sandwiches and the doctor of Norwich and get dressed and go down to eat, not in the coffee-shop but the restaurant.

Defenda me, Dios, de me! 'Lord, deliver me from myself!' If only, Teddy thought, as he dressed. If only I were not Teddy Short I would not be here, I would not be chasing Tom to Jerusalem in the crazy hope that he might be pleased to see me, give up his absurd quest and come home, to London and Bedford Row and winter and those carefully planned little dinners I cook for him that he never notices.

Anyhow, he's probably found a girl by now. Or, rather, some girl's got him.

As he knotted his tie a cold question struck Teddy: am I behaving like an exasperated friend or a wronged lover?

'Hello. Are you going the same way?'

Teddy shut his door behind him at the same moment Barbara emerged from her room. She had carried through her pledge to herself to pull up her socks and dressed for dinner.

Teddy was surprised to find that he was quite pleased to see the plain woman from the coffee-shop.

So Teddy Short and Barbara Banks went down to dinner together.

'People read too much,' Eugenia said. 'You can go mad with reading. Particularly fiction. Not that I haven't read. But I take it all with a cellar of salt.'

'A pinch, my dear,' said Fedor. He was trying to find pyjama bottoms that matched a top, gave up and settled for keeping on his vest.

'Novelists and poets are so bossy,' Eugenia was going on. 'They always expect you to see it their way and whinge if you don't. You remember when Proust came? It must have been the summer before he died. Such a difficult journey. He insisted the blinds were down all the way in the train and he had a carriage to himself.'

'No, I don't remember.'

Apart from the fact that he had lost a large part of his memory, Fedor's recollection only rarely coincided with Eugenia's time-loops.

'Such a smelly little man! I suppose it was from living in that cork-lined room. He only stayed twenty-four hours. I think he had hopes of the Arab boys but the noise gave him a migraine. And when Tolstoy was here he had shrunk already. By the end he was barely four feet tall. What do you mean, pinch?'

'A pinch of salt. Not a cellar.'

'You must have read that in a book. Fedor? What is it? Something is worrying you. Bring the hairbrush, my love, and come to bed. That's better. Now then, tell me.'

'Well,' Fedor said. He took a deep breath. 'Hamil was going on tonight about the end of the world.'

51

'Not that again!' Eugenia sighed. 'I agree these are bad times but if people would only live for the day they would be a lot happier.'

'It's different this time. Hamil says there is a portent.'

'There always is in Jerusalem. What is it this time?'

'He says the one-eyed anti-Christ is here.'

'Oh, Lord, that story.'

'You know it?'

'I had a good governess. She gave me a thorough grounding in knitting, Latin and superstition. They were promising the Apocalypse when Christ was alive. He probably believed it himself, poor soul. Not that he was a hot-gospeller like some of them. I suppose you could say he preached love and a fat lot of good that did. Of course, he was only a country boy. Fedor, you're brushing my hair the wrong way. Put down the brush. And now tell me, who is this one-eyed fiend?'

'Kalfayan the Armenian.'

When Eugenia laughed it was almost as good as Solly's cosmic roar. The bed shook.

'Kalfayan! That stinky old bugger! That pimp and procurer and miserable sodomist, the herald of the Apocalypse! Fedor, my darling, my dove, my heart, you are going to get us a brandy, then give me a smile, then kiss me.'

Fedor smiled. Then he too began to laugh. He kissed Eugenia. She was laughing so much by now that the tears were running down her face, so kisses given and received tasted of the sea.

It struck Fedor that there might be something holy about laughter.

Eugenia would not have been pleased had she known the amount of reading that was going on under her roof that night.

Thomas had left William Curthose, who was having a terrible time with the Turks and a treacherous guide who had stolen his sandals, and pulled out from his haversack the yellowed paperback copy of George Herbert.

'Love bade me welcome: yet my soul drew back/Guiltie

of dust and sinne.' He read on though he hardly needed to read, he knew the words so well. Yet twice he read and then again: 'You must sit down, sayes Love, and taste my meat:/So I did sit and eat.'

Thomas sat hunched on the edge of his bed, sharp shoulder-blades like folded wings. Never before had this most amazing of sacred poems let him down. Or, rather, he had let down Herbert, for the fault must lie in him that his attitude was not prayerful, that a face was getting in the way: the face of a girl with hair the colour of fire or fox.

Then a terrible cheap tune had somehow lodged in his head. It had arrived, as such things do, uninvited, and there was no getting rid of it: 'Falling in love with love I'm falling in love again.'

Thomas put Herbert aside, paced his room, had a cold shower, paced again, that damned tune still inside his skull. It might help if he could remember the next two lines.

What was it doing there? And, for that matter, what was he doing here? The idea of becoming a monk was ridiculous. Who would have him, for a start? And then what would such a gesture amount to but yet another hiding from the world? He had been doing that for long enough in the flat above the shop in Bedford Row. He could see it now: a winter's evening, the black English rain boiling in the gutter. Teddy pulling the curtains against the night, gossiping on soothingly about that day's customers, some wonderful library sale coming up, what they were having for supper, where Teddy had bought it and how he had cooked it.

Thomas sat down, stood up and whacked his skull on a beam. That was how he so often felt: that the world was a room in which he always banged his head, barked his shins, stubbed his toe. He had once broken a rib making love. He had stood on his sister's child's hamster. He could still hear the neat crack of the spine.

Teddy smoothed the way, he supposed, shifted the furniture out of his path, kept him from the greater accidents of life; for that he should be grateful, but he wasn't. Or not enough.

William, too, was an accident man. Thorns, literally, in the flesh. Nearly shipwrecked an hour out from Marseilles. An 'aimiable young companion' he had encountered on the voyage out, 'most sadly taken by a quaking fever' that was probably cholera. A mule dying under him. Encounter with a scorpion. Three days barefoot without a guide, his sandals stolen for the fourth time.

And so I put myself into small Dangers; a trewe Jonah to all who sail or travel with me, and all sans the Blessing of my Mother, the Church. Yet I go on in fool's hope of finding my right Lord. Still I stumble and would too gladly be at my ordinary Home in company with my sweet Wife.

Last night in a cave I shivered, and then I was Hot, and I dreamed, my Spirit low, contemplating my likely Death in this terrible land. Are these Serpents or Angels that tell me against all the words of the Philosophers, this world is not an Hospital to die in but a joyful temporary Shelter?

From this night's Spasm, I woke no more in my Senses than I was in sleeping. Almost, I would have turned back, if I could have found the Way. For in that blessed sunrise, more wonderful than we ever see in our Northern Climes, there came to me as Phantasms most real and tempting, the touch of my Wife's hand on my brow, the smell of good bread baking and the Comfort of flowers.

Thomas rubbed his head. At this point in his ancestor's pilgrimage he felt much the same as William, who would surely have understood about the fox-haired girl and the sense of total confusion that had come upon him since he arrived in Israel.

He lay down and thought of the Crusader's effigy he had seen in the English cathedral, sleeping in stone with his wife at his side and his dog, his feet crossed as the sign that he had journeyed and killed in this, the Holy Land.

Falling in love with love.

54

Thomas slept at last. But not before he heard a sound that this time was quite definitely not a car back-firing. Brakes squealed and there was the rattle of automatic rifle-fire, running feet, shouts. Danger did not cry. It barked.

Daisy, too, was having difficulty getting to sleep. She had followed Solomon's suggestion and dug out the paperback copy of the Koran she had bought at Heathrow. He was right. It was amazing. Here were Abraham and Moses, Jacob, Aaron, Jesus. And an astonished Mary giving birth under a palm tree. She liked that though it left her even more muddled than she was already.

She dipped into Runciman and read again the account of the slaughters at Antioch and Jerusalem. Such righteous butchers they were, with their bloody cross.

Daisy let the books slide to the floor. Concentration was impossible. There was too much in her head already. The fever of Jerusalem and then too many people coming and going and talking: the elusive Thomas Curtis, Morgan Pooley, Fedor (now what was Fedor doing there?), nice Solomon, that peculiar woman Eugenia Muna. And most unwelcome of all, Barbara: the voice of sense and prudence and decorum and everything Daisy found detestable.

There was a queer little half-dream that Daisy woke from, wondering whose it was. Then she turned off the light, lay down and made up her mind. The only thing to do, she told herself, is to give way to muddle.

Only the nuns that night slept the sleep of the blessed. In two rooms, four to a room (to avoid occasions of passionate friendship), they took off their flying jumpsuits in the dark and put on the sensible cotton-terylene pyjamas permitted since they cast off the habit.

Mother Matthew in one room and Sister Angelica in the other turned on their bedside lights and knelt, and the other Little Sisters of Sorrow knelt too and followed the words that were read with their lips.

'Pray for the peace of Jerusalem: they shall prosper that love thee. Peace be within thy walls and prosperity within

55

thy palaces. For my brethren and companions' sakes, I will now say, Peace be within thee. Because of the house of the Lord our God I will seek thy good.'

Mother Matthew had a hair growing from her chin and one from her nose. For her black laced boots she shopped in the men's department. She knew herself to be feared and there had been a time when she regretted this: when inside her there was a slim, dancing girl with tiny feet and a sweet voice.

The girl had never quite gone away. So while Mother Matthew, the terror of novices, snapped off the light, checking first that her charges had their hands above the sheets and one pillow only and no talking at all, she herself did not fall asleep easily. Perhaps it was coming to Jerusalem that had woken within her the girl she thought of sometimes as her soul, who was acquainted with joy, who would have praised the Lord not on her knees, but with trumpet, psaltery and harp, timbrel and dance.

In the adjoining room Sister Angelica yawned. She was beautiful and popular. She adored travel so much that every time she entered an airport she had to fight the urge to bolt to another life of ten denier stockings, silk-satin suspender belts and stretch limousines. Now and then she almost wished she had joined a Roman Catholic order where there would be no grey areas. Blind faith and hell-fire must concentrate the mind wonderfully.

Maybe Jerusalem would do the trick.

Meanwhile, she tried to pray. But it was no use.

'Anyone got a ciggy?' she said.

Fedor too was wide awake. Eugenia's brandy and consolation had put him to sleep, but only for an hour. So now he lay staring into the darkness while Eugenia snored. The only way he could get the spectre of one-eyed Kalfayan out of his head was to fill it with something else.

So he began to tell himself the story with which he had last entertained Solomon and Hamil at Magdalena's. He remembered it word for word.

'Once upon a time,' he whispered to himself, 'there was a poor boy who could not remember who his parents were.

He lived in a water-butt in a dark, cold country and worked for a farmer and his family. He slaved in the stables and the milking-shed and the fields and the kitchen. He dug turnips in the snow and the farmer's children bit him. So did the farmer's dogs but he never complained because he knew that one day his life would be quite different. One day he would live in the sun and lie in the arms of a woman who was beautiful and kind. Knees tucked under his chin in the water-butt, he dreamed of this woman, in his sleep he even smelled her and smiled, although he did not know if she were his wife or his mother or his sister – only that she would love him truly.

'One midwinter afternoon there was the sound of hoofs striking the iron land and an army rode in at a gallop, reapers of souls, slashing all around them. A grim harvest they made of the farmer and his family and every beast from tethered bull to Christmas goose.

'Only the poor boy escaped. He leaped headfirst into the water-butt and stayed there, upside-down for three days and three nights.

'Then he gathered together half a smoked ham and some apples from the cellar. He put on the rough wolf-coat that had once been the farmer's pride, shut his eyes, turned round three times, and set off south, to find his love.'

The boy diminished to a speck on the horizon, his story to be continued, and, at last, Fedor was just drifting off to sleep when shouts outside and firing snapped him back into wakefulness.

Eugenia turned over.

'Eugenia?'

'Nothing to do with us.'

As ever, Fedor envied Eugenia her detachment. To him, the killing in this most wonderful of cities was a matter to break the heart. Because of their tacit understanding not to speak of such things he did not like to ask Hamil and Solly. Eugenia always said: 'It is human nature. If Jews and Arabs had not existed they would have had to invent each other.'

Then Fedor would say, wistfully: 'There must be some solution. What would happen if Christ were to come again?'

'They would crucify him.'

Fedor covered his ears and when this did not work, pulled his pillow half over his head.

Then he was glad of the comfort of Eugenia's cold feet on his back.

'I had such a funny dream,' Daisy said the next morning. 'A cold one. I mean, it was in a cold country and there was a boy. He was hiding from something. Then I dreamed that I was in the middle of a war. I could hear the noise of it. It was weird. I dream so much here.'

'That wasn't a dream,' Thomas said. He had overslept and come down late. The indoor dining-room was full of nuns so he had come out to the terrace and there was Daisy. It would have been rude not to sit at her table again. 'Apparently some Arabs had broken the curfew and torched a car in the Christian quarter. Only a few yards from here, just inside the Damascus Gate.'

'How awful. Was anyone hurt? Were they terrorists?'

Thomas flinched. He thought of William and Syrians and Turks. He did not care to contemplate the idea of terrorists.

'Ah, Fedor,' Daisy said. 'What was that racket last night?'

Fedor looked sad and a little tired. He put down Thomas's coffee and rubbed the top of his head, the bald patch, then rubbed his hands on his apron.

'The intifada,' he said. He did not like to speak to a pretty girl of such things. Daisy reminded him of someone he had forgotten; a girl who smelled of apples and lived in the country of his dreams. He would probably never know if she were a figment or a first sweetheart. In any case, even to think of her was a small betrayal of Eugenia, though not as serious a treachery as the times his nose remembered Magdalena's armpits. 'It gets worse, I fear. The Russian immigrants. Jews housed in the Old City and on the West Bank. Zealots on both sides. Forces working from without and within.' Fedor wished he had not said that. It brought to mind the dreaded one-eyed Kalfayan. If only he were a figment.

'And who's right?' Daisy was saying.

Fedor wagged his head.

'They both are. That's the problem. That's why it will

58

go on.' Eugenia was tapping on the kitchen window. Fedor addressed Daisy earnestly. 'You must take care. If you wish, I have a good friend, Rabbi Solomon, whose grandson is a guide. His name is Gideon.'

'How extraordinary! I think I've met him. I didn't connect.'

'You have met my friend?'

'Both. But I don't really want a guide. Thank you.'

'If you change your mind.'

'Of course.'

Daisy smiled. She was amused and intrigued by the way even the slenderest of connections flung a friendly web over this amazing and confusing city. Fedor knowing Rabbi Solomon. Gideon, if it was the same Gideon. Even Thomas flitting like a lost shade through Gethsemane. Morgan Pooley, who wasn't half as boring as she had expected. In fact, quite interesting. Barbara was after him for a book, Daisy seemed to remember. He didn't look to her like a man who could finish a book.

Contemplation of Morgan Pooley reminded her that she had half-accepted an invitation to visit him this morning.

But it was so pleasant, sitting here, the sun warming her face. Thomas on the other side of the table with his nose in a book, a daring sparrow making a brave raid on the bread-crumbs. And this light. Where else in the world was there such a light?

'Where are you going today?'

Thomas jumped, blushed and knocked over the sugar.

'Gosh. Sorry. The Holy Sepulchre, I thought.'

'You must tell me about it.'

'Absolutely.'

No, Daisy thought, as Thomas thrashed away, breasting a cloud of nuns come out for the view at the exact moment he was trying to get in; no, not a monk. I don't think he'll make a monk.

'So we're both in the same boat.'

Barbara Banks met Teddy Short in the hotel swimming-pool at the shallow end. At first he did not recognise her.

59

She was wearing a swimming-cap covered in fierce-looking plastic pansies.

'Schlepping to Jerusalem,' she went on.

'Sorry?'

'I believe it means progressing with difficulty. Like Moses.'

'Ah. Yes.' Teddy followed her out of the pool. Barbara had sensible legs, he observed: table-legs. 'Actually, I was thinking of chucking it in. Going home. Too bad if they call the flight. I don't want to stay here much longer.'

Barbara towelled herself briskly.

'Oh, you can't do that! I tell you what, I've been checking on other flights. They've cut a lot because of the fuel crisis but I've found a KLM to Cairo via Amsterdam.'

'Cairo?'

'Better than nothing. Moses had to walk.'

While Fedor carried on with his work on the air-raid shelter, Eugenia and Miss Mary were having a comfortable mid-morning gin and tonic. Eugenia's was light on the tonic.

From the kitchen doorway where they sat they could see the Little Sisters on the terrace and in the garden.

'That one with the boots is stealing cuttings from your moon-flowers.'

'They won't take,' Miss Mary said.

Eugenia was wearing her football scarf today. Just because it was unseasonably hot did not mean that it might not suddenly become very cold.

She reached for a slice of Black Forest gâteau and offered the plate to Miss Mary, who shook her head.

'Never could stand nuns,' Eugenia said. 'They eat like pigs. Can't afford to turn them away at the moment. Never thought I'd miss the Japs.'

Miss Mary smiled.

'I don't think he'd have cared much for them, either. Nuns, I mean.'

Eugenia grunted. Her mind had already gone on to something else. It always moved faster on gin.

'Poor Fedor's worried about the Apocalypse. You realise Maddas is you-know-who spelled backwards? My governess

60

insisted on a close study of Nostrodamus. All the way across India. I don't take much account of him myself. Pity they didn't bump him off, though, the first time.' Eugenia rocked. 'What about a little topper?' she said, and, turning, found she was talking to herself.

That was something to which she had never quite grown accustomed: the way her only permanent lodger had of suddenly not being there.

Usually Miss Mary would turn up again somewhere quite close. A couple of times it had been a fortnight. Eugenia had been quite worried. Then a picture postcard had arrived, once from Cairo, once from the Dead Sea.

Eugenia sniffed. She often left something behind, frequently a friendly scent, musk or rose.

This time it was a small sneeze, no bigger than a cat's.

SEVEN

'**O**h, good! Here you are then.'
         'Yes. It's different by daylight, isn't it. It only took ten minutes.'
'You didn't walk?'
'Why not?'
Daisy wondered how long Morgan Pooley was going to keep her waiting on the doorstep and why he was staring at her as though he had never seen her before.
'You did ask me, didn't you?'
'Yes. Yes! Of course. Please. Come in.'
Morgan shook off leftover thoughts of the night before about Daisy and love.
'Oh, what a nice room. What did you mean, I shouldn't have walked? Everyone seems very friendly. A little Arab boy was following me. I think he was playing grandmother's footsteps.'
'Just a security fuss,' Morgan explained as he led the way. The Foreign Office is advising tourists to keep out of the Old City. Anyhow, come down to the garden. This way.'
'Oh, yes, I know. That's why Barbara cancelled.' Daisy pulled a face. 'She said she wasn't afraid for herself but she felt responsible for me. My parents are dead and she's my only living relative. Poor Barbara. I'm twenty-six and between the two of us, she's the innocent. You know her, don't you?'
'Er, yes.' Morgan changed the subject. 'Actually, that is a very narrow lane off Derech Sechem. You should be careful there. Well! Here we are.' They sat. 'There's going to be a holy war,' Morgan said.
'I'm sorry?'

For a second, or it might have been much longer, Daisy had almost forgotten Morgan's presence. She had read in her W.H. Smith guide about the dubiously alternative site of Christ's crucifixion and tomb but nothing had prepared her for the peace of the unexpected garden in this city of nervy signals. Sitting in the shade, under the tree where Morgan normally delivered his spiel, she breathed in the scents of cardamom and eucalyptus; she let her breath out, she rested. She was not certain if she believed or not in Christ and the son of God and the resurrection and the life everlasting. She imagined herself to be too intelligent, too English, altogether too C of E, for the experience of faith as anything more than a pain in the knees and a pagan shout at Harvest Festival.

And yet there had been that shadowy immanence in Gethsemane by the oil-press. And here, looking down on the screened-off grotto, a will to believe?

'D'you want to walk round?'

'Sorry? Yes, of course.'

It was simply the garden that had enchanted her Daisy decided as she followed Morgan and his cat Sheba followed them both. He pointed out the locust-bean tree and a herb upon which Sheba had settled to sun herself.

'Myrrh. Actually, it's anaesthetic. And there's the hill General Gordon identified as Calvary because it looked like a skull and skull is golgotha in Aramaic. But the main argument has always been that crucifixions were not permitted inside the City walls. See, there's the Damascus road.'

'How extraordinary! Calvary in a bus station. You know, that's funny, but it seems right. And the road's more like a souk. So much for the green hill far away.'

'John says he was crucified in a garden. And Matthew identifies it as belonging to Joseph of Arimathea. He'd have had pull with the Romans. He was a fat cat. I always rather like that bit where Mary Magdalene mistakes Christ for the gardener.'

Morgan fanned his face with his panama hat. The kind the Rev. Cuthbert Eager would have worn, thought Daisy, for an outing to Fiesole.

They sat down, Sheba jumped on to Daisy's lap. It was

very peaceful. Only the muezzin's call to prayer and the parp of the buses outside and below came as reminders that this City was not eternal, except in fantasy.

Daisy got Sheba purring.

'Where are the archeologists? You said there'd been a find.'

'Gone belting off to sniff around the competition. They've found what might be the remains of an early rock tomb inside Constantine's shrine. The Greek Orthodox don't want any digging, the Franciscans do. The usual story.'

'And here? Have they really discovered something?'

Morgan perked up.

'Well, yes. That's what I meant by a holy war. Unholy, rather. Sepulchre versus Garden Tomb. It's quite intriguing. There'd been a flood which brought down some of the back wall of the grotto. You know, Jerusalem's full of tunnels and caves and springs. Well, they came upon this whacking great granite block. And there was a fish cut into it.'

'A fish?'

'The secret sign of the early Christians. From the Greek *ichthus*. An acronym. They took some chippings away for carbon dating and it fits.'

'But if this was Joseph of Arimathea's family tomb and he was a secret Christian, then it's not so surprising, is it?'

'No, except that his tomb is supposed to be in the Holy Sepulchre. Anyway, it's enough to get the Sepulchre chaps in a tizzy: all the more since they're always scrapping among themselves. The point is, once the finding is published it will whack up our income from tourists and pilgrims. The Garden Tomb Association's very pleased.'

'And you?'

'Well, at first I thought it was quite a lark. Now I'm not so sure. You see, I rather like this place, in fact, I like it very much. The garden. I suppose that's frightfully English of me but then I am English. It suits me very well that we hardly get a paragraph in the guide books. The idea of becoming a tourist attraction doesn't appeal. Sorry, I'm rambling on rather. Do you understand?'

Daisy smiled. 'Oh yes. Yes, I understand very well.'

How odd, she thought, twice since I came to Jerusalem I have been happy in a garden.

'I knew you would,' Morgan was saying. 'You're an understanding person.' There was a sort of shimmer round Daisy, he decided, as though she had the sun behind her always. Maybe it was her hair. 'I say, can I ask you a question?'

'Depends what?'

'Are you married or anything? I mean, with someone, so to speak.'

'I was with someone, so to speak, for a couple of years. But that's finished.'

'Ah.'

She's divine, Morgan thought. So why can't I imagine the carnal bit?

'And now can I ask you one in return?'

Morgan nodded, a little nervous.

'That's fair.'

'Do you believe he's there? Was there?' She nodded towards the grotto.

Morgan was startled.

'Well, it sort of goes with the job, doesn't it.'

'But really?'

'I suppose, actually, I think he is wherever you believe him to be. Have you read the Gnostics? They're considered a bit naughty by dear old Mother Church. But they believed, roughly, in his continuing presence. That is, anyone might see him any time, in any shape.

'Have you? Seen him, I mean?'

'No. Not so much as a little finger. But in this part of the world we get several sightings a year. Though usually it's the Madonna. Flying over Cairo, that sort of thing.'

'Flying?'

Morgan beamed and nodded. Preferring gossip, he found serious conversations tiring.

'Oh, yes. Practically scheduled flights. Because the Holy Family hid in the crypt of St Sergius in Cairo after their flight into Egypt. So it makes sense. Quite fun.'

Daisy laughed. Yes, it was quite fun. What a queer country this was. A siege state poised on the edge of yet another war.

Daily threats and horrors from within and without; not that she had yet seen anything, only sensed and heard. And at its centre, this beautiful bloodsoaked city scrapping about an empty tomb. And within that city, Madame Muna's – the guest-house of dreams – and Morgan Pooley in this English garden tickled to bits about visions.

There was a shiver of birds in the weeping fig by the screened grotto. For a wonder, Morgan had stopped talking and in that golden silence Daisy had an intimation that a seemingly given truth might be no more or less than a conspiracy of imagination under the name of faith. And this didn't matter.

And whatever happened, she would leave this city not necessarily wiser, but older, sadder maybe, possibly changed.

Meanwhile it was not enough to look. She must see.

I shall go to Bethlehem, she decided, and was just opening her mouth to say so when there came a flutter of nuns down through the gift-shop door at the public gate, into the garden, scattering the birds and filling the whole air.

In another garden, Gethsemane, the three Messiahs took their ease. From here they had a fine view of the Golden Gate.

'How long do you give them already?' said the one in the skull-cap.

'Who are we to say?' said the one with the scars on his hands and feet and a deep wound in his side.

The one in the kiffiyeh sighed and pulled his beard.

'This was not my intention,' he said. 'I have been misunderstood. So have we all.'

For a while they were sadly quiet. They were used to such grief.

Then the one in the skull-cap spoke.

'Did I ever tell you, when Moses was dying Joshua asked him, "And where shall I take the Children of Israel when you are dead?"'

'And Moses answered, "Ca–, Ca–"'

'"Canaan?" said Joshua and pressed his ear to the lips of the dying patriarch and prophet, who answered him. Do you know what Moses said?'

'No. What did Moses say?'

The one wearing the skull-cap beat his forehead with his fist.

'I cannot remember! What a fool am I!'

The other two sighed.

Not another Jewish joke.

Daisy saw Morgan swept away by nuns. He looked like a man being beaten to death by butterflies.

Leaving the garden by the public gate into the narrow street, Daisy took a deep breath. She left the garden reluctantly. It might or might not be holy ground but it was wonderfully restful.

What Morgan said was true. The lane was very narrow. Daisy could not remember whether to turn left or right. Since she had no idea where she was going it probably didn't matter. On the other hand Thomas had said he was planning to visit the Holy Sepulchre and it would be interesting to compare the two sites.

It was getting hot. She pulled off her cardigan and tied it round her waist, was shading her eyes to read the map when she felt herself propelled quite roughly forward by the press of people. She looked back. Was that the Arab boy who had followed her here? A young man with a rifle, soldier or policeman, jogged her elbow.

'Lady.'

Daisy glanced behind again. If it was the boy she could not see him. An orthodox Jew walked importantly beside a primly dressed wife pushing a pram. He wore a wide fur hat, beard and ringlets. Daisy grinned: Woody Allen.

With the crowd, Daisy was carried across the main road (where did all the traffic come from, where was it going?) and had just got her bearings at the Damascus Gate when, avoiding a taxi, she turned to find herself about to be mown down by a crocodile of singing schoolgirls.

She was falling and at the same time thinking, how silly, nothing like this would ever happen to Barbara, Barbara always knows where she is going, when a small hand took hers in a remarkably strong grip.

Inside the Damascus Gate Daisy leaned against the wall, closed her eyes for a second and, opening them, saw the boy with the dirty brown face looking up at her.

'You OK, lady?'

'Yes. Thank you.'

Daisy put her hand in her shoulder-bag for some coins and by the time she looked again, the boy was going, almost gone. She could just see the top of his head, bobbing like a cork at sea.

'Come back! What's your name?'

'Jibreel, lady.'

That was what Daisy thought she heard. Then the sounds and the smells and the shadows and eternal whispers of the Old City claimed her as certainly as though a gate had slammed behind her.

Eugenia was tipping hens' feet into her stock-pot, along with cow-heels and fish-heads.

'Fedor?' she said.

'Eugenia?'

'Have we had any manifestations lately?'

'Portents. Only portents.'

Thinking of Kalfayan, Fedor double-crossed himself, once to the left, once to the right, both Latin and Easternwise.

'Are you sure? No visions? Miss Mary did leave very abruptly this morning. No mention of apparitions?'

'Nothing in the paper, my darling.'

Eugenia nodded and threw in the gizzard.

'Do we still have the carp of Urfa in the pool?'

'The sacred fish? You are thinking of cooking them?'

'Why not? Fish are for eating. I was wondering about a white wine sauce. Though you could be right, Fedor. We need a special occasion. I don't regard my birthday and you don't know yours.'

Eugenia hummed to herself as she searched among her cookery books. She had long ago given them up, preferring to cook off the top of her head with results that were sometimes amazing, often appalling. Early misuse and later neglect had left the books with spines cracked, food-stained and covered in cobwebs. Between the pages there were dead spiders, picture postcards, shopping lists and love letters.

Perhaps because he had come to Eugenia with no past to speak of and little more than the dancing-pumps he stood up in, Fedor relished her clutter. He found in it comfort and joy, something rich and generous; it was full of surprises, stories and consolations. Sometimes when he could not sleep or was troubled, Fedor would wait until Eugenia was out of the way and step into her heavy, bow-fronted boule wardrobe – a gift, she claimed, from Anastasia Romanov in gratitude for sanctuary here at some point in her life-long flight from the massacre in the basement at Ekaterinburg. Naturally, she had come to Jerusalem, Eugenia explained, since her own slaughtered sister had founded a convent here. Inside the wardrobe Fedor would snuff up the spicy, heady, theatrical, homely, sweet and sour scents of Eugenia's clothes. He would finger delicately and with love the crusty feel of an embroidered ball-gown she had worn at the Gezirah Palace when her namesake Princess Eugénie was there. He would lay his cheek against the comfort of winter flannel, tickle his sinuses with the featheriness of a boa. Once the catch slipped and he got locked in. Several hours later Eugenia heard his exhausted scratching and let him out. He had a red nose and his eyes were running. 'You are allergic to feathers,' she said. 'Dead birds are not good for you, especially in confined spaces.' Only then did Fedor notice that her own eyes were a little damp. She trumpeted largely into a duster. 'My darling Fedor,' she said, 'you are a loving fool. For a while I thought I had lost you.' After that the catch was changed and Fedor, though a continuing visitor, was never again a prisoner of the wardrobe.

'Now, where did I put it?' Eugenia was saying, pulling out the books, spilling several dead flies into the stock-pot. 'Oh well, it's all protein. So that's where that bill went. I can hardly believe I ever bought diamonds. Nasty, dull, hard things.'

A yellowed piece of paper fell to the floor. Eugenia picked it up.

'Now, here's the note from Céleste Albaret. She says M.

Proust should be offered a litre of milk a day flavoured with coffee, and will occasionally take fried sole or scrambled egg. Whyever did I keep that? I said at the time, I am not his housekeeper – such a long-suffering woman – he can muck in with the rest or go without.'

Fedor sat with the peeler in one hand, a potato in the other.

'Eugenia, what are you looking for?'

'They have been disturbing the spirits, Fedor, with their spades. All this digging. The Garden Tomb–Holy Sepulchre dispute: that is exactly the kind of controversy that brings Jerusalem nothing but trouble. What starts as an innocent speculation among diggers and probers, in the hands of fanatics can lead anywhere. And now Miss Mary has vanished. You know how she worries about her son. She misses him. She struck me as distracted. Another crucifixion or possibly a miracle would not surprise me at all. Don't they know? The dead past and to come are all around us. But when they need only look up they look down. Eyes to see, Fedor, eyes to see.'

Eugenia had found whatever she was looking for.

'Ah! Here we are. Between Delia Smith and Lescoffier. The Gnostic Gospel of Philip.'

Eugenia read briefly, snorted, snapped the book shut and put it back on the shelf at the very far end as high as she could reach.

'Well, there might be something in it, there might not. No need to trouble your head. Keep an eye on my stock-pot. I must go and search Sister Angelica's bedside locker. I suspect that young woman of venial sins. Possibly smoking.'

As soon as he was alone Fedor took down the book and opened it where Eugenia had left a dried spider as a bookmark. He read.

Jesus took them all by stealth, for he did not reveal himself in the manner in which he was, but in the manner in which they would be able to see him. He revealed himself to them all. He revealed himself to the great as great . . . and to the small as small.

70

To Fedor that made sense. If he were the Saviour he would do the same himself. Somewhere in his lost childhood he had been frightened by a plaster figure on a wooden cross, with horribly real-looking thorns and nails and wounds and blood. From a great distance he saw himself only three feet small, yelling his head off at this bleeding giant, kicking, screaming and bawling until he was carried out of this dark, humming, scented place, to be smacked. Or cuddled, perhaps?

He put back the book and wondered why Eugenia was making such a fuss.

As he pondered Fedor began to worry. Eugenia was often right about almost everything.

If there were to be a happening he hoped it would be a miracle rather than a crucifixion.

And if Miss Mary had really vanished he must water her cat and feed her moon-flowers.

Or the other way round.

'Did they say *Moscow*?'

Teddy Short had been dreaming that he was lying in bed on a Sunday morning, enjoying that delicious moment when one realises that it is Sunday, so that he could turn over and go to sleep if he wanted to, when he woke to find himself at 39,000 feet, with a crick in the neck and the captain speaking.

Barbara Banks said: 'Apparently Amsterdam is in the hands of terrorists – the airport, I mean – so we're rerouting.'

Teddy blinked. 'But Moscow?'

'There is a three-hour holding pattern over Paris, Brussels and most of continental Europe. Air-traffic control strike at Casablanca.'

'What happened to Cairo?'

'Chaos. Someone scored an own goal. Zapped an Egyptian helicopter. They're still arguing about it. Meanwhile they've closed their airspace.'

Teddy appealed: 'Istanbul?'

'Snow.'

Teddy sighed. It was surely not the right time of year for snow in Istanbul? Nor could he work out why one moment no one was flying and now everyone was in the sky weaving about waiting to land and running out of fuel. He had a mental picture of them all falling out of the sky at the same moment, big metal birds with useless wings going splot.

He shuddered. He had a dreadful feeling that he was doomed either to die quite soon or to spend the rest of his life with Barbara Banks. He had almost forgotten why he had set out in the first place.

'How do you know all this?'

'I asked, of course. I like to know where I am.' Barbara Banks was infuriatingly cheerful. 'Oh, good. Here's lunch.'

Apprehensively, Teddy peeled the foil cover to reveal his worst fears. He could have keened for his long-lost home-cut smoked-salmon sandwiches. He leaned back as far as he could, which was not very far, felt his stomach lurch and closed his eyes.

'Eat up,' said Barbara Banks. 'Then they're showing a film.'

Teddy tried not to think about Moscow. Glasnost had clearly not gone down as well as hoped. He saw himself in food queues. Fighting for a sour sausage. A long life's winter with Barbara Banks.

'Oh, look!' Barbara said. 'Is that Ararat? Or the Caucasian Mountains?'

Teddy leaned over to look and the contents of his plastic tray slid into his lap. The plane tipped and then began to vibrate as if it were trying to shake itself to bits. The seat-belt light came on. Behind him someone was kneeing Teddy in the kidneys.

All this, Tom, for you.

EIGHT

*E*ugenia always said that the most beautiful thing she
had ever seen was Mohammed on his night flight from
Mecca to Jerusalem: the small figure astride white-
winged Alborak – the mount with the woman's face and the
peacock's tail – coasting through the Milky Way and down
to the ruined Temple of Solomon. She missed him taking off
again for the gates of Paradise but she had witnessed other
wonders (and horrors). She had heard the slaughter of the
Jews by Titus and she had stood in the garden among the
women afar off when Christ cried out in the ninth hour: *Eloi,
Eloi, lama sabachthani?*

Beauty and suffering and courage, and all for what?

If questioned in weariness when her cold feet hurt and
Fedor's back was not available to warm them and she had
dropped her stitches in her cups, Eugenia would say that all
roads lead to Auschwitz or Dachau or Bergen-Belsen or the
Cross, we are all Jews. Every one of us the victim of some
almighty cock-up.

At other times, as now, Eugenia considered her unusual
capacity for receiving audio-visual messages and decided it
was a freakish gift (or curse) about as useful as being able
to stand on your hands.

For instance, whatever use was it, she thought, as she
watched the scummy fat rise from the ox-head she was
boiling for supper, to have such a queer talent and lack the
skill to direct it? She could give an eye-witness report on
the destruction of the second Temple. She could see Daisy
Herbert taking the wrong turning in the souk, wondering
whether to buy a blue necklace made of stone chippings
pretending to be turquoise. Yet she could not find Miss

Mary. She could smell one-eyed Kalfayan scuttling after his dirty business but she could not raise so much as a finger to save this damnfool city.

Fedor heard her sigh. It was unusual for Eugenia to be despondent but he knew what to do when she was.

'Come, my darling, you have been on your feet too long. You are making too much cooking. Let us lie down.'

Neither of them undressed completely. Fedor took off his shoes and belt and arranged the silk cushions exactly so. He smoothed the under-sheet and when Eugenia had lain down, pulled off her oiled-wool socks, warmed her feet with his hands and kisses and then covered her with the wonderful quilt that Miss Mary had made for them years ago. It was a magical quilt because it consoled always and because it changed. One day it blazed with birds – peacocks, their necks entwined with blushing flamingoes – the next the appliquéd motifs might be of the many branches of one tree and every kindly leaf a jewelled eye.

Once he had crossed the shutters and drawn the quilt up to Eugenia's chin, Fedor himself slipped into bed beside her.

It was a still, early afternoon of tremulous gold. From the City below, a single bell spoke in a hopelessly romantic voice that said gravely and sadly: peace, peace.

Eugenia sighed for a second time.

'If no one had ideas,' she said, 'this place would be perfect. But then, I imagine, it would not exist.'

Eugenia's rare melancholies were like no one else's. Fedor had long understood that there were afflictions worse than a forgotten history. There could also be too much of remembering.

He kissed Eugenia on the cheek, on the mouth and then on the mouth again and she kissed him back and at last she smiled. The afternoon was hot and Fedor had to think of snow to keep down the rising in him. Down, Magdalena! An eternity of love above the waist with Eugenia is worth anything to be had in the secret café! Concentrate on a white Christmas! It can snow in Jerusalem!

'Dear Fedor,' Eugenia said, 'you always cheer me up. And the carp. You know they are older than anyone, than

74

anything? They are almost older than my memory. They are older by thousands of years than Christianity or that new-fangled Islam. It is said that they were born of the fire-brands with which Nimrod would have slain Abraham but it's my opinion they go back further than that in other parts of Mesopotamia. Perhaps to the very beginning. If there were a beginning. Myself, I believe time to be circular. They were taken from a sacred pool by my Turkish great-great-grandfather – a famous poacher – not by hook or line but in a golden net it took fifty virgins five years to knot. The fish are said to answer to their names if one happens to know them. And there is a story my nurse told me when I could not sleep or cried in the night, that one of them wears a golden jewel on his upper fin.' Eugenia smiled and squeezed Fedor's hand. 'Sometimes I cried when I was perfectly happy, so that I could have the story again and the carp would swim through my sleep. Poor Fedor, I have told you this tale before.'

'Never.' Fedor crossed his fingers under the quilt.

'You are a liar, my dear, but a kind one. And I am thankful to have them at last in a proper fish-pool. I hope you are feeding them well, Fedor? But not growing too attached?' Eugenia's voice was sleepy. She yawned.

'Crumbs and lentils,' said Fedor. He considered the other part of Eugenia's question. Although they were unusually gleaming for carp, golden even, a fish, however sacred or magical, was a fish. It might be worshipped or eaten but not loved. Besides, he could do without the weekly chore of cleaning the pool. And he was always worried about Miss Mary's little cat. The fish looked big enough to swallow it, ancient shadows glowing with their own gold at the bottom of the pool.

Eugenia yawned again. But Fedor was puzzling.

'If they are holy fish how can we eat them?'

'It can be a sacred act to eat sacred flesh.'

That was true. From Fedor's long past there swam up a voice speaking a language he did not know but understood: 'This is my Body, this is my Blood.'

Fedor had never had such a long conversation about fish.

But clearly, the carp – or, rather, the eating of the carp – had some special significance for Eugenia. Once a year she talked about cooking them but she never did.

'When shall we eat the carp, Eugenia?'

'Before too long, I think. It could be quite soon. A very dull fish though. We'll need a strong sauce.'

Her eyes closed. Her voice trailed off.

Fedor feared and hoped. Might the great carp-eating mark consummation? Or Apocalypse? Or both? In which case, in what order?

He opened his mouth to ask but Eugenia was snoring already. She had put herself to sleep, speaking of her nurse's story, and was swimming through that most death-like of all sleeps, the siesta, in company with a carp, who had a name and wore on his upper fin a golden jewel.

A few steps in from the Damascus Gate, Daisy thought she should turn left for the Moslem quarter, right for the Christian. Hesitating, since both looked the same, she paused in front of a kiosk and decided: it would steady me to buy something ordinary, I have always wanted a turquoise necklace.

When a voice in her mind said, 'Don't be silly. They're painted stone,' Daisy jumped then handed back the necklace, shaking her head. To her surprise, the Arab merely shrugged and as she walked on she was struck not only by the narrowness of the streets, which she had expected, but by the fact that even though she had come this way with Thomas last night, she recognised nothing and there was no landmark from which she could get her bearings.

Outside the walls, looking over the City from the Mount of Olives, Daisy had seen the pharaohnic architecture of the grandiose new hotels, the determined roads, the neatly planted gardens. That was another country of harsh light, another story, permitting no ambiguities. Here, inside the City, was a world of plots and sub-plots, remembering, grudgeful stones, confusing echoes, old secrets and new graffiti. Much of the wall-writing had been painted over but Daisy noticed a caricature of a hook-nosed Jew, a crescent, a star of David.

Was that the Arab child playing grandmother's footsteps behind her? And where had everyone gone? The crowd at the Damascus gate had vanished. If people lived behind these walls and iron shutters, there were few of them to be seen. In a cave-like interior two old men were playing a board-game while a third watched, drawing on a hookah.

Every moment, Daisy realised, she had been expecting to meet Thomas but the deeper she went into the City the less likely it seemed that she would find him. She began crazily to wonder if she would even get back to Madame Muna's. She felt light-headed and for half a second almost missed Barbara, who would not only know the way but would have stoked up both of them with a sensible Israeli breakfast. Barbara never lived with hopeless men in a damp London basement. Barbara arranged the world to suit herself and avoided the parts that might not. Barbara would take the Moslems and the Jews and the Fundamentalists of all kinds, and bang their heads together. Barbara actually believed still in the possible conversion of the Jews. Barbara must be written to tonight, without fail.

Allowing her cousin to enter her mind for that brief moment steadied Daisy. She blinked and quite suddenly she had a bearing. There, just above, was the small square with the high wall and the gate leading off, where she and Thomas had looked at the moon last night. To her left would be the Via Dolorosa, and round the corner, surely, the Holy Sepulchre.

Yes, there was Jibreel waving to her to come on, hopping from one foot to the other. And the nuns – Daisy recognised the beautiful one and the one with outsize feet in black boots. They looked rather wonderful in their white head-dresses, somewhere between a coif and a scarf, bobbing and nodding like feeding birds.

'Lady, lady, I lost you!'

'I lost myself, Jibreel.'

Daisy was standing in a triangle of sun in the yard outside the church, laughing at the boy, who laughed back with delight, when she heard someone speak her name.

'Miss Herbert? Daisy?'

There he was, Thomas, looking flustered and hot, nearly strangled by his camera strap.

'Sorry,' he said as a ferocious young back-packer in studded leather stood on Thomas's foot.

Then he told Daisy: 'I got lost. On the Via Dolorosa.'

Daisy had been right about plots and sub-plots. Outside the City the light was hard and dazzling and dangerous. Armies sweated in the deserts and there was the sound of wars past, wars present and to come. Near Jericho in time present nine Israelis died in a grenade attack on a tourist coach headed for a luxury hotel on the Dead Sea. Elsewhere, Palestinian mothers called to their children: throw no stones, our house is broken and our hope gone, come away, come away.

Within the walls iron-age tunnels and Ottoman drains threatened the City with terminal subsidence. Hamil Ibn Abbas Sartawi, minor imam and patron of Magdalena's secret café, who came not from the desert at all but via Cairo's al-Azar University, Amman's blue-domed mosque and similar postings, heard for the one thousand and first time his wife Hamida's screeching plaint for a bliss she considered lost the day she was removed from her father's household above and behind the perfumery favoured by the best noses in Cairo.

Hamida's liturgical reproaches were voiced with the predictable regularity of daily prayers. You could set your watch by them and once a month you could be sure that in Hamida's creative nostalgia yet another room would be added to her father's establishment, another ancestor to the family's pedigree.

Even in his moments and days of greatest weariness Hamil chose not to contradict Hamida. He believed that her condition sprang directly from their childlessness and for this reason never contemplated taking another wife or divorcing Hamida. Privately, he suspected his father-in-law to be a purveyor of hashish along with the essences of jasmine and sandalwood.

'Oh, for the house of my father where I have respect!' Hamida wailed.

78

Hamil sighed and wished his heart were not so tender. Once, on Solly's advice, he had called her bluff. He had even bought her ticket. 'Go,' he had said, 'go to your father, with my blessing.' But Hamida had switched at once from shrieking to sobbing and temporarily lost the use of her legs.

If Hamil had not been a man of passion as well as tenderness, he might simply have made a quiet life for himself outside the house, at his duties in the mosque, in chess and talk with Solly and Fedor. He might have worried a little, but not too much, that in the words of the Prophet it is written, he that Allah hates shall remain childless. But there was within him a man of violent feeling who would have loved greatly, one in whom love divine in its most corporeal expression could have imitated, in marital sensuality, nothing less than the love of all right-thinking men for Allah and Mohammed his prophet.

It was this divine and frustrated sensuality that had somehow been blocked, twisted and turned to rage. Seeking an object, this anger had wandered for a while, gnawed his gut, this rat-rage, until it settled at last, most terribly, on the one-eyed anti-Christ of Hadith knowledge: Kalfayan.

Hamil cracked his fingers, pulled on his outer robe, closed the door with the knocker in the shape of Fatima's hand, and made his way through the narrowest streets and deepest passages of the Moslem quarter. He crossed the Via Dolorosa and made himself no more than a narrow shadow flicking through the complicated honeycomb that led to Magdalena's.

So mad he was, so possessed by visions of Kalfayan garrotted, poisoned, crippled, crucified, for the first time in his life he forgot that he should be at the mosque preparing for five o'clock prayers. All he felt was relief that Solly, at least, was there.

The rabbi looked up from his plate of sweetmeats. Magdalena and the mynah bird were watching a soap-opera on the television set at the corner of the bar. Fedor arrived half a moment after Hamil, panting. The messenger from Hamil calling him to Magdalena's had spoiled his siesta and annoyed Eugenia. Fedor felt as he always did when he had to

79

leave their bed of loving friendship unexpectedly: tormented by the thought that had he stayed that might have been the very day when Eugenia would have woken in the mood for consummation.

Even the equable Solly was irritated.

'Hamil, my friend, this is the second time you have called us together in this way in as many days. Normally we never speak of such things but with our peoples set against each other there can be little peace for either of us. We must look to their care. We must restrain the zealots. These are bad times for all of us and for Jerusalem. And you are even thinner. Have you not been eating? Are you ill?'

'In my heart only,' Hamil croaked.

'The Armenian again?'

The imam nodded.

Solly continued: 'I have said already that you are by yourself in this.'

'I know,' said Hamil. 'But I need your wisdom.' He hunched his shoulders and the other two bent to hear him. 'While I am set on destroying him I fear that in doing so I may commit a terrible sin. Worse than blasphemy! Were I to destroy him I would be taking upon myself the sacred role of Isa, as it is foretold.' He wagged his long yellow head. 'Such sacrilege.'

Fedor was getting a crick in the neck from sitting between the two. He longed for a glass of angels' pee. He looked wistfully in the direction of Magdalena but failed to catch her eye. She and the mynah bird appeared to be discussing the soap-opera. 'What rubbish!' Magdalena was saying. 'Can't she see he's the wrong man? Look! His eyes are too close together.' The bird moved along its perch, flapped its wings and said something like 'Awk!'

Solomon was saying brusquely: 'If you are so troubled you should be consulting the mufti.'

Again Hamil wagged his head. Minor imam and Koran scholar he might be, but in his mind's eye Fedor put his friend on a camel and watched him gallop away to join his ancestors eating goat in the desert outside a black tent. Oh, for the days when the only contention between Solly

80

and Hamil was when one backed Karpov and the other Kasparov!

Then Fedor jumped twice.

First there was the sound of an automatic rifle not far away. Then Hamil slammed his hand down on the table so hard the glasses on the bar complained and the bird said 'Awk!' again.

The glitter in Hamil's eye was both triumphant and possibly mad.

'My friends, I have it! I have the way! I see clearly now! All will be well, inshallah!'

Patiently, Solly asked: 'Can you tell us what you have seen?'

'It has come to me! For the second time a bird has told me the way! First to send me on the hajj. Now to reveal to me in the voice of an angel, Allah's will.' Hamil's expression was transfigured. 'I am a tool. Allah works through me. I rid the earth of the one-eyed imposter and save mankind from Armageddon!'

Fedor felt quite dizzy.

'You mean the mynah bird? I thought it said awk?'

'In the words of the Koran, apostles have been called sorcerers and madmen. The Day of Judgement is still certain. But Allah, the compassionate, the merciful, has spoken to his miserable servant. May his will be done.'

Whatever mad notion Hamil had, it had cheered him up. He looked almost sane. His face cleared, he held up his hands in a prayerful gesture. His gaze embraced his friends.

'Now my way is clear. Here only,' he said, 'in the whole world, in your company, in this place, there is consolation. And peace.'

Fedor rubbed his stiff neck and smiled tentatively, a nervous, early-morning sun.

Solly relaxed and beamed.

'To that, my dear friends, let us drink!'

'OK, boys,' said Magdalena, one hip hoisted suggestively. 'What'll it be?'

And while Daisy and Thomas were trying to make sense of the Holy Sepulchre, within the same walls, only yards from where they stood, one-eyed Kalfayan scratched his piles and lit a Turkish cigarette. The smell of priest was too much.

Kalfayan was used to haggling with anyone who came to him with a proposition. He had struck deals with the opposing zealots of KACH and Hamas, with Mossad, the CIA, the KGB, with gentlemen from Istanbul bearing illegal white substances.

Nothing, from an abortion to an assassination, was too small or too large for Kalfayan (provided he got his commission). As the most successful middle-man in Israel, property was his present speciality. He had front companies in Panama and Lichtenstein. He prided himself on his dispassion. Jew, Christian, Arab or donkey, it was all the same to Kalfayan.

As he flicked the dust with his silk handkerchief before accepting a claw-armed chair, Kalfayan reflected that the pre-1967 Jordanian occupation of the Old City had marked his salad days, when no secret was too small to sell. Now, however, with the flood of Ashkenazim from the East, the growing dissension between Israeli and Arab and the appetite of Jewish hard-liners for property in the City, Kalfayan considered his high summer had come.

Not that he had put aside ambition. Everyone had his dream. Kalfayan's was to sell the Mosque of Omar to the highest bidder.

One day perhaps, one day.

Meanwhile, he adjusted his black silk eye-patch, ran his fingers over his amber worry-beads, and took the measure of his compatriot and latest petitioner. He was always entertained by the rivalries between the various keepers of the Sepulchre. This one appeared to be a particularly hysterical specimen: his hands shaking as he poured the Turkish coffee.

Kalfayan waited for the grounds to sink.

'I don't normally make house-calls, you know. Don't you ever clean this place?'

Cobwebs were everywhere. There was not so much as a grille to let in daylight. A single bare bulb flickered. The smell was of incense mingled with body odour.

The Armenian priest talked. His teeth were yellow. Kalfayan's were gold.

Kalfayan flicked the dust of ages from his sleeve. He listened. He nodded. He shook his head. He sighed.

'You are asking me to steal a fish from the Garden Tomb?'

'Or deface it. The method is unimportant. You, of all men, must know of a way.' The priest had the breath of a camel. 'You will understand that the Sepulchre cannot afford to lose revenue to the so-called Garden Tomb.'

If there was one thing Kalfayan understood, it was revenue.

'Very well, it shall be done.' He took his pocket calculator from inside his jacket, made a few sums, then presented his final addition. 'Half on the table, half on completion. I trust we are not Arabs to haggle.'

They finally arrived at the figure Kalfayan had had in mind from the start.

'Dollars, not shekels. Or a direct deposit to Geneva.'

The priest flinched, tugged at his beard and finally nodded. He made to shake hands. Kalfayan offered his finger-tips, quickly withdrawn.

As he was about to leave the priest spoke again.

'Not a word of this, of course, to the Patriarch.'

'Now, that will cost extra.'

Altogether, a very satisfactory deal, Kalfayan considered. He had been paid three times in two days for the same job: yesterday by the Greek Orthodox and Catholic churches, today by the Armenian. The war between the guardians of the Holy Sepulchre had proved very much to his advantage.

As might a real war, he reflected. Not for nothing did he have fingers that reached even to Baghdad and Damascus and Tehran.

This City makes fools of the wise and martyrs of the innocent. So in this country of the blind, the one-eyed man is king.

Which reminded him, the socket where his eye had been brought stabbings of quite unexpected pain. And neither catamite nor whore could coax to life that part of him that was sick. Kalfayan could have choked on his own lust.

That evening Kalfayan lay on his couch in the apartment off Ararat Street but he could not rest for visions of downy boys. He was most particularly tormented by the memory

83

of one he had not thought of for years: a street-boy like the rest, in Marrakesh, no beauty and a little lame, but Kalfayan had, for a brief time, felt for the hungry child something unfamiliar and disturbing. He had put it out of his mind for years because love was not a sentiment he entertained. It disgusted him.

Sweating, Kalfayan got up to close the shutters. Around him the air seemed to blow both cold and hot.

Below, in the corner of the yard, Hamil hissed, clicked his teeth, spat, and pulled his robe around his face; and as the rectangle of light in the window of the false prophet was put out, turned away and himself joined the many shadows of Jerusalem.

Upstairs, behind the shutters, Kalfayan called.

'Boy, bring the whip!'

NINE

'Fedor?'

Eugenia woke in an unusually good temper from her fish-filled siesta. In her dream she had swum alongside the jewelled carp, knitting as she swam, her hair streaming behind her. From a fish-eyed view, she had seen the rippled face of her father, smiling and stroking his moustaches while round the pool and round again, the ties of her starched white apron flying, ran her nurse carrying the silver-backed hairbrush.

And then she spoke and the carp answered and told her his name. Eugenia was not awed nor surprised.

'I saw you die,' she said.

The fish answered.

'They will eat my body and drink my blood.'

Eugenia nodded.

Swimming and knitting, knitting and swimming, she laid her cheek against the flank of the golden carp.

'Where have you been, Fedor, my dear? You are out of breath? Ah! No need to ask. I smell musk. So how is Magdalena? Don't worry, I am not upset – I had such a good dream. I think we might have a little party. That girl with the extraordinary hair has been in my head. I thought at first she was of no account, but I have changed my mind.'

Fedor sighed and sat on the edge of the bed.

'I am worried about Hamil. I'm afraid he might be going mad. Did you say a party?'

'That doesn't surprise me. He won't be the last. My governess was always very hot on Millenium studies and Apocalypse fever. I had a test every morning through one

85

whole winter in St. Petersburg. That was before the revolution, of course.'

'Of course,' Fedor nodded, even though he had never quite grasped the principles behind Eugenia's skimming-dish journey through space and time. If one took time seriously, as by the clock or the calendar, it would appear that on more than one occasion she had been in three places at once.

Not that he could talk. He had mislaid his own history. For all he knew, he had never been born.

Eugenia was going on: 'It was the same at the time of Christ. Prophecies, miracles, shooting stars, Romans. People expecting the worst usually get it. Did you know that at the beginning of the fourteenth century the Baltic Sea froze over twice? Doom-mongers and fanatics – there'll be more where Hamil came from.'

Fedor sighed. 'You mean he-whose-name-shall-be-spelled-backwards was not the last?'

'The mad ass of Mesopotamia? I'm afraid not, Fedor. Not the last by a long chalk.'

In a blink of an eye Eugenia smelled plague, heard the dry rattle of locusts, the cry from Arabia Perdita. But she was accustomed to such unlooked-for visions. They were out of time and for all she knew, had already happened. They came to her as a sneeze might, between chopping-board and stove, a knit row and a purl.

No point in making Fedor more anxious than he was already.

Eugenia smiled. 'Don't look so worried. We have each other and the carp in the pool. I have forgotten a lot but I know you are the only man I ever loved.'

Fedor took her hand.

'Is that really true?'

She put her hand on his cheek.

'Fedor, my darling, I would not wish to live without you. Now, we must go down soon to put on the dinner. Lentils, I thought, with the ox-head. And tapioca pudding. First though, a brandy for me and a vodka for you. Empty your head of everything that happened at Magdalena's and I shall tell you about my wonderful siesta.'

So Fedor closed the shutters, poured the drinks (a treble, as usual, for Eugenia) and made himself comfortable on top of Miss Mary's quilt, beside Eugenia. And he stopped frowning and listened and his face cleared and he began to smile as Eugenia related the story of her swim with the golden carp.

He gave a little sigh of satisfaction as she finished.

Then he asked: 'Was I there?'

'Of course. You were swimming beside me. You always are.'

Tonight was the night of what Madame Muna called her little reception.

Daisy wondered who would be there and what to wear.

First though, there was the letter she had been putting off for days.

'Dear Barbara.'

Daisy yawned, doodled an elaborate flower on the cover of her writing pad and thought how impossible Barbara was to write to.

Never had Berkhamsted, England, Barbara, Thursday meetings at the library, seemed so far away. Not that she disliked the library or her job there. Barbara said she was throwing away her degree but Daisy liked being a librarian. A lot of it was boring, of course, but she loved the smell and taste of books and words. She also quite enjoyed doing things that annoyed Barbara.

But even Barbara was so distant now. Perhaps it was Jerusalem, perhaps it was Madame Muna's, but ever since she arrived she had felt strange, at once liberated and somehow possessed. In half-sleep, on waking, there came into her head intimations of something like eternity. Words, half-heard from a conversation in another room. Love. Death.

And faces. A face. Thomas, looking lost in the Holy Sepulchre. The hissings and whispers and weight of faith (or fantasy) in that place that was at once so awful and so haunting. Grubby, more like a bazaar than a church, grim with age and thick to suffocation with the words in many tongues of those who had brought their dreams and pain into that grotesque candled darkness.

Another figment. The grey ghost she could not have seen in Gethsemane. But the extraordinary peace of that garden – Daisy felt it would stay with her for the rest of her life.

And then there was Jibreel. Or perhaps she made too much of him, too. Maybe, coming here, you saw what you wanted to find, which did not mean to say it was real. The gunshots (offstage, so far): they were real. So was the Arab who spat when she looked and turned her head away. The Israeli taxi-driver, manic-depressive survivor of the Yom Kippur war and the Lebanon, took both hands from the wheel and laughed: 'Jerusalem is crazy! Half a million people, one million cars. I tell you, all crazy!'

He swerved to a halt outside the City walls. No man's land, he said, a concrete wall when the Jordanians held the City. A shopping centre was to go up here. Meanwhile there was nothing, an earth-mover dozing.

Daisy picked up a copy of the *Jerusalem Post* she had found pushed under her door and put it down again. No time. She could hear, from downstairs, the comings and goings of the preparations for tonight's party – if it was to be a party. Normal dinner, Fedor had told her, was to be replaced by a buffet, except for the Sisters of Sorrow, who would eat early.

Daisy decided to wear the blue silk shift. There might just be time to wash her hair. First though, Barbara.

She screwed up a page of writing-paper, threw it into the wastepaper-basket, and began again.

My dear Barbara,
I do hope you are not still worried. Take no notice of the papers. Truly, everything is fine – wonderful weather and this really is the golden city!

Seen so much and so much still to see, most of it will have to wait till I get back. So far, I think you'd like the Church of St Anne even more than the Holy Sepulchre – so simple and lovely in a garden of pepper-trees and acacia. In fact, you'd be surprised by the gardens here, so much green, and water, even a forest – though the Jews say the Arabs burn down the trees.

You were afraid the Israelis would be rude but everyone I've met has been so nice. A sweet Arab boy called Jibreel has appointed himself my unofficial guide – or, rather, he keeps bobbing up every time I get lost, which is often. And your Morgan Pooley *so* kind I hadn't the heart to bring up the book he's supposed to be doing for you. I will, when it seems the right moment.

Madame Muna's pension a bit odd but *very* respectable. A party of nuns. I bump into them everywhere I go. Hope to meet Madame herself properly tonight.

Time I got ready! Must go. Do hope the weather isn't as awful as it was when I left.

Daisy shifted in her chair.

Dear Barbara. I wish we could talk properly sometimes. You've been so kind to me but I'll never be the person you want me to be. And I suppose neither of us can alter, which is sad.

All the same, this comes with my love.

Daisy.

Before she could change her mind about the last paragraph, Daisy folded the letter and sealed the envelope.

Then she heard a familiar cry from below – Madame Muna calling: 'Fedor!' It was a top C and her pitch must have been perfect, for the small chandelier in the centre of the ceiling shivered, and one single crystal drop cracked in half and fell.

It wasn't Moscow. That at least, was certain, Barbara decided.

'How do you know?' Teddy Short said glumly as the plane made a hideously bumpy landing, more like a belly flop. Teddy had listened and was half-convinced that he had not heard the undercarriage lowered. It must have been, though, because there they were, wherever that was.

'Because the name of the airport is not in Cyrillic.'

Barbara tried to wipe the small aircraft window with her

hand but of course the rain and the dark were outside. Across the tarmac above a huddled scrawl of buildings, a blinking sign spelled on and off: CRJZBC. 'Eastern Europe though.'

'How can you tell?' Teddy sneezed. His eyes pricked, his throat tickled, his limbs ached. He could no longer remember why he had set out. He felt that he had been on this journey all his life. Or, rather, that this eternal voyage was his real life, the other a fantasy.

'All consonants.' Barbara peered. 'It looks as if we have to walk. No sign of a bus.'

'I think I've got a cold.'

'Bad luck,' Barbara said cheerfully. As Teddy stood she humped down the hand-luggage and struck him on the head. 'I say, I do hope it isn't one of those Baltic republics.'

Rubbing his head, Teddy followed her down the aisle.

'Baltic what?'

'You know, the revolting ones.'

Teddy didn't know. He didn't care. He traipsed after her to the terminal building. It looked more like a public lavatory. The rain had turned to hard, angry hail.

Indoors it was no warmer than it was outside. For sixty people there were four plastic chairs, bolted to the ground. An old woman, furious looking, appeared to be making a half-hearted attempt to sell garlic. Possibly they were in Transylvania. Her twin sister, equally angry, guarded what must be the wash-room, judging from the smell.

Teddy shut his eyes. He thought of England, Bedford Row, flu, his three down pillows, the electric blanket, aspirin, whisky, even Tom's appalling scrambled egg. Especially Tom's grey scrambled egg. Especially Tom.

Barbara came back.

'There's canned Diet Coke but no hot drinks and nothing to eat unless you fancy raw garlic. What a good thing I got my thermos filled on the plane.'

'You did?' Teddy looked at Barbara with something like admiration.

'And there should be a flight to Ankara, though they can't say when. From there our best hope seems to be Amman.

90

Then we have to improvise, since Jordan is non-speakers with Israel.'

'Does someone speak English, then?'

'No. Not even French. Just those absurd consonants. But if you insist on information it is amazing how you can get it.'

'Well, I suppose we'll be more comfortable in the transit lounge.'

'This is the transit lounge.'

'Ah.'

Teddy sneezed. Barbara surveyed him.

'What you need is aspirin and whisky. Both of which I happen to have. Just as well I keep my medical kit in my hand-luggage.'

Half an hour later, woozy with aspirin and whisky and fever, wrapped in a prickly grey blanket Barbara had bartered for by buying the old witch's entire stock of garlic plus bonus, Teddy said: 'You are a remarkable person.'

'Not really. I'm quite ordinary. I have no imagination, you see, so I just carry on. I'm afraid I often irritate dear Daisy. My fault, not hers.'

'I think I'm lucky to have run into you.'

'Yes, we do seem to suit each other, don't we. But I suppose you're gay, aren't you?'

'Am I?'

Dawn did not break. It just stained the black windows grey.

The concrete floor heaved with bodies attempting to sleep. Even Barbara looked exhausted.

Mentally, Teddy reviewed their impossible journey, the mounting folly of this pursuit.

'What are we doing here? Why do we carry on?'

'Because we love them,' Barbara said. 'Rashly. For it is not as if they love us.'

Leaving the Holy Sepulchre with Daisy, Thomas had said: 'You don't think we're being followed?'

'No. Well, yes. Sometimes. But there's no one there. Except sometimes Jibreel – he keeps popping up.' Daisy looked at her watch. 'It's not late. Would you like to go on for a bit?'

They sat down and Daisy took out the map.

'We can't be far from the Dome of the Rock. But there's no entrance marked on the map and I haven't got my guide-book. Then there's the Wailing Wall and the new museum in the Citadel. Oh dear, there's so much, isn't there?'

Thomas nodded. He wasn't really listening. Instead he was admiring the halo of light behind Daisy's head. It seemed to be given off by her hair.

In the end they settled for the Citadel and afterwards sat in the garden enclosed within the walls.

Daisy stretched. Her feet were sore and her back ached. Although the air was cooling there was still heat in the late afternoon sun.

'I thought the Sepulchre was horrible. All that liver-coloured marble. A priest tried to sell me a candle. What did your William make of it?'

Thomas appeared to have wrapped his long legs around each other twice. Daisy hoped he wouldn't try to stand up.

'He hated it,' Thomas said. 'He called it a filthy nest of Popery and superstition. The friars tried to make him pay to kiss phoney relics. He wrote that he preferred Moors and Jews. In fact, he liked the Jews. He met quite a few, mostly merchants.' Thomas uncrossed his legs and folded them under his chin. 'Actually, it's rather a mystery. He had this vision, you see. A sort of revelation, I suppose. That is, he *saw* Christ. What I can't make out is where. It couldn't have been in the Holy Sepulchre.'

'What happened to him then? After the vision?'

He tried to get to Mount Sinai but didn't make it. He mentions the Dead Sea. And the Red Sea. There's some marvellous detail. Good travel-writer's stuff. It's not clear what happened in the desert. Just that he set out for Sinai and came back but hardly a clue about how he got on in between. A few lines – they sound a bit mad.'

Daisy nodded.

'Did he get home?'

'Yes. He came out of the desert. He went back to Jerusalem and then to England, four years after he had left. His hair had turned white. But he's very touching about his wife and family and going home.' Thomas's knees cracked as he unfolded. 'I say, I don't usually go on like this. Must be boring.'

'No. Quite the opposite. I'd love to see the journal some time.' Daisy glanced upwards. The museum was cleverly laid out so that you could only walk through one way but every few yards you emerged onto the inner rampart, giving on to the garden. There were the nuns again, pointing to the garden and the statue (fibreglass?) of a mounted Crusader.

'I used to think the Crusaders were so romantic,' she said. 'Not any more. Saladin was a gent, though. Did you know the story about Kerak? When he attacked there was a wedding so he laid off the tower where the honeymooners were.' She shivered. She wanted to stay but it was too cold. 'They slaughtered the Jews.'

In a story Thomas would take her hand and she his. Almost, they did, but this was life.

So William watched and Jibreel, and the other wandering spirits, as the dusk drove Daisy and Thomas from the garden.

And by the oil-press, under the olive tree in Gethsemane, the Messiah who wore the skull-cap, woke. He laughed and threw up his hands.

'I have remembered the joke!' he cried. 'What Moses said to Joshua!'

But the one with the wounds in his side, his hands and his feet, had gone. And the other was snoring, his kiffiyeh pulled across his face.

Yahweh was disappointed. But he had not the heart to wake him.

'A what?' Daisy said with difficulty. Madame Muna had produced the most peculiar canapés – very hot and very hard. They were vaguely the shape of hens' feet. And there was something odd about the wine, as if it had been spiked. Her head was swimming already.

She saw Thomas on the other side of the room and waved but he was trapped against the wall. Somehow the Little Sisters of Sorrow had got into the party after all.

She had to bend to hear what Fedor was saying.

'Did you say a vision?'

Fedor nodded. He was wearing a shiny black suit that had seen much better days and had greased down his hair with something that smelled like lard.

'It was in the paper this morning. And on television. The wife of an Arab cobbler in Bethlehem had a vision of the Virgin. She came to her door as a pilgrim and asked if the woman had seen her son.'

'But how do they know she wasn't just what she seemed – a pilgrim?'

'Because she drank a glass of water and when she had drunk the glass was still full. And her feet didn't quite touch the ground. Such a relief for Eugenia!'

'A relief?' Daisy was puzzled but before she could ask she heard a familiar voice and turned. 'Morgan. I didn't know you were coming.'

'Absolutely never miss Eugenia's parties,' Morgan said. 'If only to see what she's wearing. Look, isn't she fabulous? I always think she's the mother god in the Gnostics.'

'Incredible.'

Eugenia, advancing upon them now, was wearing an amazing peacock-coloured silk tent with turban and feathers to match. She allowed Morgan to kiss the tips of her fingers, then took Daisy by the arm.

'Come, my dear, this way, or those terrible nuns will be upon us.'

Am I drunk, Daisy wondered, or is the room actually moving? It was a not unpleasant sensation, like standing on a gently heaving deck. Then as if the room were breathing. And there was a wonderful smell of flowers.

What pretty feet she has, Daisy remarked to herself.

Madame Muna was saying: 'I have been thinking about you.'

'You have?' The turquoise necklace she did not buy came into Daisy's head.

'I may be wrong but I think you are a rare person. You have clear eyes. But you are confused. Am I right?'

'Well, a bit. I suppose what I feel is that the more I see the less I understand. All the talk about love – the love of God, the sort we sing about in hymns, this beautiful city. Then there's so much fear, and hate, it gets in the way. Or perhaps that is the truth? I'm just a naïve Englishwoman. I try to be a good tourist. Maybe I've come at the wrong time.'

Madame Muna nodded. 'I would say we are close to a bad time. I could be wrong. Time is relative. I do despair myself. I sometimes think, if these Arabs and these Jews could lose their memories, they might live in perfect peace. You know, Moses married the daughter of a Midianite priest? So Yahweh may have been just another desert god. They are more alike than they are different, these peoples. As are we all. The villain is history. Our idiocies become history. That dung-heap. In that horse-shit the worm memory breeds: cause of half our troubles. And in this land remembering is a sickness.'

Eugenia blinked, as if on waking, and put her hand on Daisy's knee. Her rings, one of which she had on every finger, flashed signals – ruby passion, emerald ice, eye of tiger. Round her neck she wore a golden torque, clasped in front by two serpent heads, which writhed, winked their jewelled eyes, then with a hiss, settled again.

'And yet you know,' Eugenia was saying, 'it is wonderful how much we still have in us of the angels. Considering the fall. Those like the angels, like Fedor, without memories, are the truly innocent. And even for the rest of us there is still the possibility of love. Of flesh or soul, that is not important. Love abides.'

'But what is it?'

'A talent. Like knitting. Nothing to do with all that mushy stuff poets moan about. You've either got the gift or you haven't. I'm talking about the everyday stuff, of course. Ah, Morgan, there you are. Take Miss Herbert outside. She looks

95

flushed. And leave the doors open. I'm feeling the lack of air myself. Too many nuns.'

Daisy had really wanted to talk to Thomas. In fact, she realised, she very much wanted both to talk and to listen to Thomas. But it was like Jerusalem itself: one set out and at every turning there was obfuscation. Look and ye shall not find. Or you will find something you were not looking for or expecting.

It came to her, as she took a deep breath of the night air, that this was a journey, a city and a country of invisible frontiers. She had looked at the map to identify the borders of the occupied territories but none were marked.

'I say, excuse me,' Morgan said. 'There's the Bish.'

Morgan nipped off in his white-rabbit way, and as someone spoke her name Daisy looked round, expecting Thomas. But there was Gideon, the guide from the first day. The grandson of that nice Rabbi Solomon.

'I didn't know you knew Madame Muna.'

'Everyone in Jerusalem knows Eugenia.'

They stood by the pool. Gideon smiled. He looked much more attractive, Daisy thought, as handsome as she had remembered him but less stern.

'I can call you Daisy?'

'Of course.'

'A pretty name. A flower.'

'I don't like it much. My parents got it from Henry James.'

Gideon wore the usual Israeli short-sleeved shirt, no tie. There was something very distracting about his forearms. And his lips. And his narrow hips. I am not drunk, Daisy thought to herself. I am simply tired. I have Thomas in my heart and my head. But it is a long time since I went to bed with anyone. Which has nothing, necessarily, to do with love.

'I have brought you a book,' Gideon was saying. 'Hebrew poetry.'

'Thank you.'

'So where have you been?'

Daisy told him.

'And Yad Vashem?'

'What's that?'

'The holocaust memorial. Not far. You must go.'

'If you say.' The earth had steadied and so had Daisy. 'Actually, I want to go to Bethlehem. Perhaps you can tell me how to get there?'

'You should not go by yourself. I could take you. I am afraid it will not be what you expect.'

Something obstinate had settled in Daisy's mind. She had suddenly had enough of stiff-necked Israelis, this siege mentality, those bloody shirts. Madame Muna was right. This country was sick with history.

'You mean politics, I suppose. They don't interest me.'

'Bethlehem is in what you would call the occupied territories. The West Bank.'

'Then why does your Israeli guide-book call it a town of happy Christian Arabs?'

Morgan had reappeared. Gideon said: 'Miss Herbert wants to go to Bethlehem.'

'Jolly good,' Morgan said. 'I say, it's rather fun, isn't it?' He was talking to Daisy. Quite rudely, really, excluding Gideon.

Daisy smiled. 'What's fun?'

'The vision. The Virgin. What we were talking about the other day. It's happened.'

'Oh yes, of course. Fedor seems very excited.'

Then Gideon left and the party ended, the lighted room emptied and, watching Fedor snuff the candles in the deep window-sills, pinching them between forefinger and thumb, Daisy lingered on in the garden with Morgan, who for once had stopped talking.

Then Daisy sighed. She took in a cooling breath of eternity, looked out at the lights of West Jerusalem and the darkness to the East, and thought she had been unkind to Gideon.

'I know I shall feel quite different in Bethlehem,' she said. 'Bethlehem will be better. Morgan, tell me about Madame Muna. Are she and Fedor married?'

'I don't think so. Though they're certainly a couple.'

'Who was Mr Muna? What sort of name is that?'

'It means something like beautiful in Arabic. Actually, I'd guess the Madame's honorary.' Morgan lowered his voice. 'No one's ever got the full story. It's rather queer. Fedor says he met her in Cairo and Fedor couldn't lie if he tried. She told me once about her childhood in Turkey and as you can imagine, I was dying for more, but you'll never get anything out of her she doesn't want to say. But the point is, no one can remember when the pension wasn't here in Jerusalem and Eugenia running it. There's a story that Lawrence mentioned her and it in the original draft of the *Seven Pillars* – the one he lost at Reading station. There's not a soul – except perhaps for Fedor – who knows how old she is.' Morgan grinned. 'She's a one-off, Eugenia. She ought to be monstrous but she has the kindest heart I know.'

Daisy felt something furry brush her ankle.

'Oh, look, Miss Mary's cat. I saw Fedor feeding it so it can't be hungry. Maybe it's missing her.' Daisy picked up the cat and it hung on, purring. 'Morgan, about the visions. D'you know anyone who's ever seen him? Here, I mean, in Jerusalem?'

'Christ? No. No, I don't, not actually. I say, are you all right?'

'Yes, thank you. But I'm looking forward to Bethlehem. I know that will be different.'

Daisy nodded and thought to herself: it will be quite different in Bethlehem. I know.

Eugenia groaned. She allowed Fedor to help her from her dress and to take off her turban. The feathers made him sneeze and remember his imprisonment in Eugenia's wardrobe.

'My head!' said Eugenia. 'I talked too much and left that poor girl even more confused. I know what will happen. She will go to Yad Vashem and weep, they all do, even the guiltless, and she will probably be disappointed in Bethlehem and I cannot see the rest. And even if I could, there is nothing I can do about it.'

'You can come to bed, my darling,' said Fedor. 'At least we need no longer worry about Miss Mary.'

'That's true. Oh, Fedor, my head is so hot and my feet are so cold.'

'This turban is too tight. There, now your head is cooler already. And I shall warm your feet.'

From Eugenia's head-dress a peacock flew out of the window. Miss Mary's cat, crouched by the carp pool, watched it fly, higher than any peacock had ever flown before, up above men and beasts and stars, as high as paradise.

TEN

*I*n his room, Thomas examined the card he had found
pushed under his door. On the front there was a sepia
picture of folk-dancers in some kind of national dress.
The thin men wore high, crotch-splitting black trousers, the
fat women black boots, laced bodices and vast precarious-
looking head-dresses in the shape of crossed fish rampant.
The women held ribboned tambourines and the camera had
caught one of the scissor-legged men, having jumped or been
thrown, in mid-flight a good five feet from the ground.

The lamp started to blink. Another power cut on the
way.

Thomas turned over the card. On the other side there was
his name and address in Teddy's writing, uncharacteristically
large and scrawled capitals.

Of the message, Thomas could make out only a few
words: WE ARE, TRANSIT, and HELL. The rest looked as if it
had been either censored or smudged by rain. Either way, it
was undecipherable. Only the postmark, upside-down above
the florid stamp (crossed fish again, a stag and a castle), was
clear to read: CRJZBC.

After the party and the peculiar drink and the embarrassing
attentions of Sister Angelica and not having had anything to
eat since breakfast except for a hen's foot, the implications of
the postcard were too much. In the first place, Teddy was
obviously not in Bedford Row. Transit suggested flight,
which meant that Teddy, who never flew, had taken to the
air: a desperate step for which the motive must have been
imperative.

It was just possible, Thomas supposed, that Teddy had
decided to follow him to Jerusalem. But if so, what was

he doing in a place with no vowels? Who were WE? Where was HELL? Was Teddy drunk? In jail? Being tortured? Gone mad?

Thomas shook his aching head, winced, sat down on the hard chair at the small writing-table Fedor had found for him, and thought he had been struck blind.

Of course, a power cut. He groped for the candle and lit it. He would worry about Teddy in the morning. Meanwhile, he was looking for a passage in William's journal.

Here he was in the South Sinai desert:

in the Company of Angels and Prophets and Fiends. I am much troubled for I cannot divine if these are Semblances of sand or Creatures of my mind. In my former days as a Skeptic, I would have held all such Manifestations to be no more than Phantasms; but then, although of middle years, I was in the Childhood of my Spirit, when all that I received through my senses or my Intellect was measured against the rule of Reason.

Now, since my Bowing in the City of Christ Crucified, I apprehend the words written by *Sir Thomas*, the Physician of Norwich, when he speaks of the Adorable Mystery.

So, although I am lost in these dreadful sands, even though I die here and may never again see my dear wife and touch her sweet cheek, but leave my bones for vultures, I consider myself the most Fortunate of men: lost that I might be found.

William's tone in these passages was not always so high-flown, nor as reconciled to whatever fate awaited him. In the course of one paragraph he complained about the heat of the day, the cold of the night, sores and fluxes, 'an issue of blood' from what must have been agonising piles.

'There are occasions like this,' he wrote:

when my Adventure in this desert appears to me the most convincible Folly . . . but then I feel the strong hand of *Joshua* on my shoulder and I see the Children of our first Fathers, *Moses* and his company, who are

101

as the Bedouin in their desert wanderings. I hear their voices, see their camp-fires at night, their black tents; am given my Reveille at dawn by the harsh cries of the women driving and herding their cattle and long-horned goats.

Then it comes into my mind that my Peregrination is not so much through this fearful Sector of the Earth as through Time itself.

So, lacking yet the Wisdom of that Hero, I am as *Prometheus* freed by *Herakles*. Unchained from our Present Days in their sweetness and corruption to make my way sans chart or wits, dull as a dung-beetle, tossed upon these Sands like a mariner in a Tempest, without compass or direction.

Should these notes be discovered in the litter of my bones, take them, Traveller, not to Churchmen who in these days are Skeptics all and would deny as Heresy, no doubt, both these reflections from the Sands of Time, and more surely even, my suffusion of joy at the Apparition of our kind Lord; who shewed Himself to me not in Glory but more as that good Man and Poet, *Mr Herbert*, might have acknowledged: in Simplicity; though not among Thieves but as a Gardener. In a place that will be a Garden by a Tomb that is in a Cave and not yet recognised.

Give them instead into the keeping of my Widow. And let her do as she will. Offer them to other Travellers with the Admonition that sand will long have covered my tracks and they might best stay at Home. Tell her that we may be Resurrect in our own lives. That is, wait not on Death. Our souls may leave our bodies before the mirror is no longer misted, and while I may lie with her in bed or in the grave, my spirit might be encountered any day in Jerusalem.

Tell her to marry again. In the words of *Donne* (which I misremember) before soul into soul may flow, it must to body first repair.

Say to her: publish my strange Tale or weep, as I know she will, and burn or closet them against Pinchers, Stealers, Cricks and Masters of Divinity. Best of all, let her cultivate her garden and press flowers between these leaves, if they are not already Dust.

The wind blows from the north. There will be a sandstorm before dark. *Hic locus terribilis est . . .*

In the preface to Thomas's eighteenth-century edition the editor surmised that William had either run out of writing materials – charcoal, presumably, possibly parchment – or temporarily lost his senses.

It was the second speculation that interested Thomas. He must have read the journal a hundred times but in this section, before the sequential break, he always went back to the same phrases: 'lost that I might be found.' And 'Resurrect in our own lives.'

So close was William tonight, that Thomas felt the light touch of his hand on his own shoulder. The candle guttered, the door creaked, the small high window blew open then shut again.

He dreamed he was asleep, then that he was the child he had been in the lonely Oxford garden. Mother resting, then gone, like a bird in the night. Father among his fossils. And every Christmas the aunts said: who will have Tom this Christmas?

Thomas woke hunched over the desk with a crick in his neck and a full moon slopping at the window, and heard the words he had overlooked so often, the clue, the key, the pointer, the answer so well hidden in plain sight: 'In a place that will be a Garden by a Tomb that is in a Cave and not yet recognised.'

Of course! It fitted with the Gospels. Why should General Gordon have been the first to identify the place of skulls? And now there was the fish Morgan Pooley had been talking about. When he came to think about it, it was perfectly obvious.

Wide awake now, Thomas stood. He banged his head on a beam and was still rubbing his skull when twenty minutes later, after a trot through empty streets, he stood before the private gate in the wall of the Garden Tomb. No point in trying the door to the gift-shop and this one would certainly

103

be locked. He could hardly knock up Morgan Pooley at this time of night.

Normally, Thomas would have been windy of walking the narrow streets of the Old City at night. Certainly he would have been alarmed by the wail of what sounded like a siren.

Tonight though he was possessed. What he expected to find in the Garden Thomas could not have said. But William was in his heart, his head and his hand: the hand he raised to the gate that must be locked and yet opened to him. A sign, surely? A faerie gate beyond which he would discover, as in story, the answer, or at least the clue to the answer to a great secret.

The hinges must have been oiled because the gate swung to silently behind him. And there was the Garden, silver-milky with moon, darkness deepened, trees and bushes etched.

And over there, in the tomb, was that a light? Forgetting the way, Thomas stubbed his toe, tripped and must have called out, for when he looked again the light was gone.

He proceeded more cautiously from the higher level of the Garden to the lower. His eyes had adjusted to the night and he could make out quite clearly the weeping fig. From there he could feel his way to the tomb entrance. He had to bend double to enter and was just reaching into his pocket for the torch when he felt a crack on the back of his skull and along with his senses, the moon, the lonely small boy he had been, the foolish pilgrim who had come to Jerusalem to find William or Christ, or to lose himself, he could not have said – all were eclipsed.

Fedor sat bolt upright in bed.

Eugenia mumbled.

'Fedor, it's the middle of the night. What's the matter? Indigestion? I warned you not to eat the hen's feet.'

'Wasn't that an air-raid warning?'

'Yes. But it's a false alarm. This time.'

'You mean, next time it will be real?'

'Probably.' Eugenia turned her pillow the other way up. 'Now go back to sleep.'

'How?'

'Come here. Let me put my arms round you. Now, breathe with me and we shall dream together.'

'I can hear the nuns looking for the air-raid shelter.'

'Let them look. Now. Close your eyes. There, that's better.'

Fedor often thought that although Eugenia had denied him access below the waist, no woman could have been more generous with her spirit. He had fallen in love with her forever at the moment he had glimpsed her exquisitely turned arch in Cairo. But it was the first time that she took him into her dreams that Fedor truly grasped this was a woman like no other in the world.

The joys of a Magdalena – or, rather, specifically of Magdalena herself – tempted and troubled him. But such brief ecstasies would be as nothing beside the rapture of his soul-wedding with Eugenia. The dreams – if dreams they were – in which they leaped from their bodies as easily as you might rise from a chair, and each with an arm around the other's waist, swam in ancient pools or flew high to the hyacinth-scented music of the seventh sphere, from there to look down on earth.

The sights they saw! A caravan in Arabia. Armies. Deserts as sweet as a woman's tawny hair on a pillow. Themselves, mouth pressed to mouth in the bed in Jerusalem under Miss Mary's magic quilt. And once, Eugenia pointed to the northern hemisphere, a little to the east. 'Look,' she said, 'there you are. Upside-down in the water-butt.'

Tonight, however, Eugenia's loving ploys failed. An hour later Fedor was still awake.

'Was that a knock? I heard feet.'

'Mother Matthew's boots. I imagine she has lost Sister Angelica. That girl smokes. She was flirting last night. She's probably done a bolt. Why don't you tell yourself your story?'

'I tried. It didn't work. I'm stuck. I thought they were having a peace conference.'

'They are. Now, Fedor, dear, your hands are cold. You are shivering. Camomile tea? Or perhaps a little cognac?'

'Something is going to happen, isn't it?'

'I expect so.'

Eugenia had the brandy, Fedor the camomile tea.

Still Fedor could not sleep.

So Eugenia told him a story, one he heard before, the better to send him to sleep.

'You remember how my governess taught me, and I told you, that the soul may live outside the body and yet the body not die?'

Fedor nodded and Eugenia went on with the tale of the beautiful girl, Bidasari, whose kindly adoptive father put her soul for safe-keeping into a golden fish.

'He hid the fish in a pond. And for many years there it stayed, until the wife of the King of Indrapoora heard tell of the beautiful girl. She grew jealous, captured her and tortured her, until Bidasari begged her to take the golden fish and bind it round the neck. Then she would die.

'Are you asleep yet, my darling?'

'No. Go on.'

'I think your lids are heavy. Well, the Queen did as Bidasari said and the girl fell into a swoon. She sent her home to her parents. By day, when the fish was out of the water, Bidasari lay unconscious. That was how the King, out hunting, found her. By day his kiss would not wake her. But when he came at night, when the Queen put the fish back in the water, Bidasari was awake and told the King all that had passed.

'And then the King took the fish from the Queen and put it in water. So Bidasari was herself again and the King took her for his bride.'

Fedor wondered if someone in his lost childhood had told him stories. He found them deeply comforting. Also, he had no great difficulty in telling stories to Solly and Hamil. Maybe he was not really telling but remembering?

He closed his eyes. He opened them once to ask Eugenia if by any chance Eugenia had put his soul and her own in the golden carp in the pool. And, if so, what would happen if and when they ate them.

But Eugenia, in telling the story, had put herself to sleep. The cognac had probably helped.

Tenderly, Fedor drew up the quilt to cover her shoulders. By the time the all-clear sounded, both were snoring.

In the night City many were awake.

In Bethany Martha called out to Mary: 'Sister, what is it, the sky wails?'

'It's only thunder. Not the end of the world.'

'Are you sure? There are other signs of the last days.'

'Hush. You'll wake Lazarus.'

'He is afraid to sleep, our brother.'

'It is the grave he fears. Though he need not.'

'I wish our Master would come. He favours you.' Martha bit her lip. She had large, rough hands made for washing. Mary was the beauty. She could sit on her hair. She could have married any time she liked.

'He will come back, but not until Passover,' Mary said. 'Now go back to sleep.'

This time, instead of upstairs rooms with windows sealed against poisoned air, the inhabitants of Jerusalem were digging deep, discovering that the foundations of the City were not as solid as they had imagined. Of course, everyone knew about Hezekiah's tunnel and the shaft to the Gihon spring, and that there were more caves and more shafts, together with an Ottoman water and sewage system. But few had any idea of the City's deep and complicated substructure.

They were finding out now, and in the face of what might turn out to be the most devastating assault since the massacre by the Christians in 1099, they prepared to take grateful refuge in the entrails of history. The Jebusites turned and grumbled in their long sleep as the opening of tunnels and the shoring-up took place. Revealed were springs unmarked even by the Israeli authorities, graves, treasures of time, cellars and secrets.

Deep under the King David Hotel the American Secretary

of State, in jogging suit and track-shoes, was trying to keep up with his opposite number in an aerobics work-out.

It felt to him as though he had spent the last ten years commuting at 39,000 feet between Jerusalem, Amman, Tehran and Damascus. There were times when he had difficulty remembering where he was. And now this air-raid warning.

He tried to keep patient. He did keep patient. But it was always the same old story. Resolution 242 in permanent suspension. Land for peace but not yet. Jerusalem non-negotiable. The now historical, heroic restraint of the Israeli state in the face of Saddam's provocation.

'Yeah, Dan, I know. But you've got to remember I have to talk to these Arabs.' The Secretary was sweating and panting. Someone handed him a glass of orange juice. He hated orange juice but that was Israel. 'If you could just lay off the Lebanon for half an hour then we'd be talking turkey. And you know as well as I, the West Bank settlers are not pioneers. They're assault.'

The Secretary was now pulling up what breath he had left from somewhere round his balls. It was never like this for Henry Kissinger. Negotiation was supposed to be a subtle, dignified affair. For Godsake, he'd seen tapes of himself looking subtle and dignified. He'd been on the cover of *Time* magazine way back. Those were the years he'd held his belly in and no one had to hook him into a corset before he'd even taken the first piss of the day.

'Dan,' he gasped, 'why don't we just sit down a little bit?'

Even when Dan Dare relaxed, his deltoids and his pectorals and the iron muscles of his diaphragm stayed on alert.

The Secretary was weeping sweat.

Tachycardia tapped at his ribs.

He heard the all-clear through the piped communication tube.

Maybe, after all, if he lived through this night, he would not die in a lead-lined bunker in the bowels of Jerusalem.

So he prayed, allowing himself to look forward to the comparative paradise of Cairo.

And he heard in his head the Washington prayer, whispered every morning by the faithful in the State Department, through time immemorial, though never aloud: 'Dear Lord, please make Israel go away.'

Listeners even more secret than Mossad monitored the heartbeat of the representative of the greatest power on earth. Their microphones were so finely tuned, from West Jerusalem they could hear a donkey fart at the Dung Gate.

They needed to listen, for in this City there were enemies within as well as without.

Only three places had they failed to bug: Madame Muna's (some static interference from eternity), Magdalena's (they had no idea it existed), and Kalfayan's.

So they did not hear the nuns running up the stairs and down the stairs looking for the air-raid shelter. Nor did they hear Daisy get up when the siren woke her, open her door and close it again. If there were really any danger she felt sure that Fedor would come and get her.

But there was no point in trying to sleep yet, she knew, although, oddly, the possibility of danger did not disturb her. She had no idea why, since she had never considered herself brave. Barbara said she was irresponsible but Daisy didn't believe that either.

In her white cotton nightgown, with the full moon staring through the small window, she curled up on her bed with her books, even her flaming hair, washed silver and blue.

By the light of the moon Daisy read. Vaguely, she thought she must talk to Thomas tomorrow about Donne's *The Ecstasie* and Herbert's *Love* and the way the more she read, the less precisely drawn did the line appear between the secular and divine, body and soul, sex and God.

She was probably being simple minded. She was reading subjectively, in the wrong mood.

Next to hand on her bedside-table was Gideon's rather surprising present: the thick paperback of Hebrew verse.

An hour later she rubbed her eyes. It was amazing. Expecting to be lost in an alien culture, Daisy found herself responding again and again to images, to beauty, to an everlasting longing three thousand years old and yet of this very minute. From the Song of Deborah and Barak to the very end, among doves and golden islands and mulberry trees, in exile and power and peace and war, she recognised these voices as though she had always known them, and remembered what Rabbi Solomon had said: something about standing back far enough and seeing that everything is the same.

She skipped, of course, dipping, and it came into her mind that she was peculiarly susceptible to poetry – indeed, to words – and the bustle of daylight might turn all to flicking shadows, dead petals, scattered ash.

Near the very end, long after the all-clear, one voice spoke from a sealed freight car:

> Here in this carload, I, Eve, with my
> son Abel. If you see my older boy,
> Cain, the son of Adam, tell him that I

Then Daisy might have cried. But the last of Herbert's blessings – weariness – closed her eyes and stopped her tears.

Meanwhile, there was another voice the listeners failed to hear.

Kalfayan, in the lowest intestine of the organism that was the Old City of Jerusalem, in his deepest cellar below Ararat Street, clutched his empty eye-socket with one hand and with the other struck his incompetent thug across the cheek. His heavily ringed fingers broke the skin.

'Fool! Idiot! Son of ass and dog!'

He sighed and reached for his map of underground Jerusalem, drawn up over many years. At least, whatever he caught or stole, he would never lack for a place to hide it.

'Put the Englishman there,' he said, jabbing the map with his thumb. 'And now out of my sight. Imshee!'

Alone again, Kalfayan considered this unforeseen circumstance. There was doubtless some way he could turn it to his advantage.

His mood improved. After all, the night had not turned out too badly. They would have found out by now that the air-raid alert was a false alarm but it would still be enough to sabotage the peace talks until he could think of some other device. There was the money to come from the parties interested in the fish. The Soviet immigrants were getting daily more unpopular and desperate for a roof over their heads or a ticket and visa to some other destination.

Plenty of pickings.

And he was always consoled by his wonderful chart: the maze of subterranean limestone quarries, underground chapels, ancient quarry shafts, medieval staircases, water cisterns.

Old Jerusalem was like a man who lived with his foolish, dreaming head above ground, unaware of his lower life, the secret City, his buried fundament.

As dawn broke over Jerusalem, high in the Judean Hills, in Shepherds' Field, a woman in blue wandered. Distracted, she might have been taken for crazed Isis or Demeter. She was neither and she was both. She was all women who have sustained a great loss.

It was the wrong time of year for spring flowers, even for poppies, but there were a few to pick of those that go by the name of the day's eye. There is a hybrid also that appears at Michaelmas.

Her feet did not quite touch the ground. Yet the hem of her skirt was wet with dew.

ELEVEN

'*T*his is Ankara. When they've refuelled we can take off again but we can't change planes,' Barbara said.
'Why?'

Teddy did not really want to know but felt he had to ask because Barbara wanted to tell him.

'There seems to be a riot. I never did understand Turkey. I do hope we don't have to go back to that place with the consonants. Oh, there's someone getting on – that girl with the baby. Poor thing, she does look tired. It's wrapped up so tight you can't see its face.'

Teddy winced. Barbara's aspirins and whisky had internalised his cold, so that he no longer sneezed, nor did his nose run. Instead, his whole skull felt swollen and his scalp stretched too tightly to contain it.

If only he could keep quite still and very quiet. Every sound hurt and to turn his head was agony. He did so very carefully in Barbara's direction, as a man might balance a fish-bowl on top of his head, from which not a drop must slop over.

She had defied the instructions to keep seat-belts fastened and was now returning from one of her information-gathering forays.

'Moscow again,' she announced. 'Meanwhile strap ourselves in and no one to pee. Cheer up. There are worse places than Moscow. It might have been Crjzbc.'

'What did you say?' Teddy whispered.

'Crjzbc.'

'About the loo. I rather need to go.'

'I'm afraid you'll have to rise above it. Think of something dry. Deserts.'

'I've never seen a desert.'

'You're the one with the imagination. Imagine one.'

Teddy closed his eyes. All he could see were waterfalls, gushing fountains, dripping taps.

'It's not working.'

Barbara looked at him.

'I'll see what I can do.'

She was back in three minutes.

'You can use it if you don't flush.'

Teddy made a dash. Literally relieved, he lowered himself again into his hard seat. His head was still a fish-bowl but it didn't hurt any more.

'However did you fix it?'

'I said you had a serious kidney condition.'

The plane that had brought them from Crjzbc was very small. From his window-seat, Teddy was quite sure he could make out a hairline crack in the wing. The stewardesses looked like those nurses you see in films of provincial Russian hospitals. They had big jaws, purple lipstick and massive hands. Smiling had been omitted from their training manual. They glowered threateningly as they handed out newspapers that had come aboard along with the girl with the baby.

Barbara got one in what might have been Turkish. Teddy got an English tabloid.

It was mostly about football stars, pop stars and television soap stars. Also the Royal Family (SHAPE UP QUEEN TELLS BIMBO FERGIE). Confessions of a drag artiste concerning a member of the cabinet (GIRLIE GAMES WITH MINISTER IN PEEPHOLE PANTS). A bingo page. Then one small paragraph on an inside page Teddy had missed the first time he flicked through.

'Oh dear. I say. Look at this.'

He pointed. Barbara looked.

ISRAEL AIR RAID THREATENS PEACE TALKS.

'How old is that paper?'

'Today's. It must have come out on a morning flight.'

'Well, nothing we can do about it, is there? They are both totally irresponsible or impossibly innocent.'

In flight again, even Barbara seemed disinclined to talk.

Then she said: 'We do get on, don't we. Rather a pity you're gay.'

113

'Are you sure I am?'

'Oh, yes.' Her tone was matter-of-fact. 'It's quite all right if you are. We're both in the same boat, in a way.'

'You don't mean – '

'No, I'm not, as it happens. But, you see, I'm behaving as if I were Daisy's mother and you as if you were Thomas's wife. We're going where angels fear to tread and if we ever get there, they'll probably resent us. Not that we have any choice. We are what we are, so there's no point in brooding about it. It will be interesting anyway. Did you know this is the year of the Mission to the Jews?'

Teddy shook his head, wonderingly.

'A mission to do what?'

'To convert them. Think about it. If Israel went Christian.'

'I'd say the C of E would have a problem.'

'You might be right. One can only press on and hope for the best.' The engines were so noisy Barbara had to shout. 'There's something peculiar about that baby. Have you noticed, it hasn't cried once.'

'Perhaps it's asleep.'

'Possibly.' Barbara dug in her bag. 'I say, I'd forgotten. A pack of cards. Never travel without them. What about poker? Or pontoon?'

'I'm afraid card games aren't really my thing. I only know Happy Families.'

'Extraordinary. You must have had a queer upbringing. We can't play Happy Families with this lot.'

'How about Snap?'

The vibration was appalling. Teddy's head was beginning to hurt again. And his stomach. He didn't want to play anything but Barbara had already pulled down the tray from the back of the seat in front and was dealing the cards when, across the aisle, the girl with the baby stood up, snatched away the baby's shawl and began to scream.

'What is Madame Muna doing?' Daisy asked Fedor at breakfast.

She was sitting at the window that gave a view of the lower

114

terrace, beside the fish-pool. Madame Muna was wearing an outfit that looked like pictures Daisy had seen of Winston Churchill's siren suit – an all-in-one garment in some thick dark-blue stuff with a buttoned placket at the back for obvious purposes and a zip up the front.

'She's giving the nuns gas-mask drill,' Fedor said. He had slept late and was wearing his pyjama jacket under his apron. He too, looked down. It was an odd sight: the six women in their coifs all bobbing and nodding in their rubber snouts.

'Why the nuns particularly?'

'She doesn't like them. I'm afraid she can be rather naughty sometimes. I do hope the air-raid warning didn't disturb you? It was a false alarm.'

'No. I mean I heard it but nothing happened so I guessed it was all right.' Daisy smiled. 'You love her very much, don't you, Fedor?'

'Oh, yes! For me it is the greatest thing, the love between us.' Fedor spoke shyly but his face was transformed. 'Sometimes I am afraid,' he confided. 'But I know the truth is, such love as ours is proof of eternity. Indeed, Eugenia says we are in eternity already.'

'That's wonderful, Fedor. I envy you.'

Even more shyly, Fedor said: 'But you, Miss Herbert? You have a friend?'

Daisy shook her head.

'No, Fedor. I have never known anything like that. I doubt if many people do.' She pushed the flakes of croissant around her plate. The sun turned a corner and flooded the dull, cream-painted room with pure gold. A golden coin lay on the surface of the blue milk in the white jug. Daisy realised that she had woken unaccountably happy this morning. 'I mean, people want to love and be loved so much, they use the word as a name for all kinds of feelings that are not love at all. I wish I knew how you can tell.'

In a moment that was not unlike the orgasm she had woken with that first morning, Daisy thought she caught a scent of hyacinths that were not there and then the sound of doves calling and a single bell bronzely ringing.

115

And when she looked again the nuns had gone and so had Fedor.

She finished her coffee and considered Fedor's confession. Really, it was like saying God exists because I have faith.

Well, why not?

Today, it appeared that everyone was going to Bethlehem.

The nuns were milling in the lobby, demanding a minibus to take them to Bethlehem. Anglican scruples tossed overboard, they were hotfoot after the reported manifestation of the Virgin.

But this was the great Jewish holiday. Minibus drivers, along with most taxi-drivers, were either booked or themselves taking part in the festival.

Fedor telephoned with no success. Then he nipped out, around the maze of streets, and came back with a small open lorry on its way to Bethlehem to collect vegetables.

So what the military helicopter saw as it flew south, checking the road to Bethlehem, was a smaller than usual stream of Christian pilgrims, among them a party of nuns clutching at the struts and thumping up and down in the back of a lorry.

They also saw, but did not note, a dirty old Citroën with curtained windows, inside which Kalfayan hung on to the strap and cursed every time the barely sprung vehicle lurched from side to side and up and down. One paid a price for travelling incognito. But if there were anything in this Virgin business the Armenian wanted his cut of the cake. Besides, the keepers of the Basilica were overdue with their protection money.

And then, driving with some dash, overtaking both Christians on their way to Bethlehem and Jews heading for Rachel's tomb, was a small cream convertible with the top down.

'That looked just like Morgan Pooley. I wonder if it was.'

Daisy peered after the cream convertible. It was trying to overtake one of those alarming Israeli white security vans, which shrieked like ambulances and seemed to contain never less than half a dozen ferocious giants.

116

To her own surprise, Daisy was sitting beside Gideon in his four-wheel-drive desert jeep. She had imagined him in a tank. She had imagined too, that she would be setting out for Bethlehem in company with Thomas, who had not answered when she knocked on his door, nor come down to breakfast, nor left a message.

At traffic lights she turned her head to catch a glimpse of another van, this time with an open back, like a lorry. She saw two figures, Arabs, lying as though they had been flung there, arms tied behind their backs. One had a makeshift-looking blindfold over his forehead. The other saw Daisy and she saw him. The lights changed and the van pulled away. There had been something in the man's eyes. Despair, bravado, but also a kind of mocking invitation that said, look, this is how it is, how I am. He was like an angry animal in a zoo. And in some way, he was shrugging his shoulders. Daisy wondered: this is nothing to do with me, not my fault, so why do I feel shame?

Gideon had appeared that morning, just when she had given up on Thomas and, since Bethlehem seemed too complicated, was trying to decide what to do with her day.

She said: 'Shouldn't you be guiding people somewhere?'

'It's a holiday. The last day of Succot. The Feast of the Tabernacles. A celebration of the end of the year's reading of the Torah. Anyway, you may have noticed, there's an emergency on. Trippers have flapped their wings and flown away.'

'Succot – that's a sort of harvest festival, isn't it?'

Gideon laughed. Daisy wondered how she ever could have thought of him as fierce.

'You've been talking to my grandfather. He's very hot on pre-Judaic faiths. You know: Christ as Osiris, Jung, universal archetypes. You think all a rabbi does is wail and moan, don't you?'

'Well. Not exactly. I mean, I didn't know. It would be impertinent to pretend I did. And what about you?'

'Me? I'm a sabra. I was born in the Land. My family came here in 1875. The first of the great experiments. Most

117

gave up. Ghetto Jews from Eastern Europe, they were urban idealists. They couldn't cope. But we hung on somehow. And here I am.' Gideon pulled off the road and braked. 'You'd better see Rachel's tomb.'

Gideon was waiting for her.

'Well?'

'It seems a bit sad, somehow. Little scraps of cloth everywhere. So small. And packed with people – you can hardly breathe. Those women.'

'They go there when they can't get pregnant. To pray for children.'

'Do you believe in that sort of thing?' Daisy asked.

Gideon shook his head.

'I'm secular.'

'I'd no idea.'

'Oh, there are plenty of us. Well, here you are, Royal David's City.'

He was watching her. Was he laughing at her? Outside the Church of the Nativity there were a few half-hearted-looking Arab touts, tourists who might or might not be pilgrims. Carols sang in Daisy's head, incongruously. There is a green hill far away. Constantine's church was handsome. Everything else sad, confusing or awful. Hanging censers decorated with tatty Christmas balls. The usual liver-coloured marble. The manger more like a hole under a table. She had read, none of the guardian priests of quarrelling faiths could agree about reroofing, so the Israelis had done it.

And yet in the Grotto a woman knelt to kiss the silver star, so naturally, with something like hunger. O, come all ye faithful.

The whole place, the town itself, appeared to be empty. Or, rather, shutters were down, doors closed. They had walked first round Manger Square. The souvenir shop was shut. Glancing up, Daisy saw snipers on the roofs.

Partially blocked by the Turks, the door into the Basilica was forbiddingly small. A rectangle of darkness.

Joyful and triumphant.

Fantasy? All this? Jerusalem too? The whole thing? There was no evidence, after all, that any of them had ever lived,

118

from Abraham to Christ himself. Daisy had known this when she came here. She regarded herself as a rational person, sharp, vulnerable to poetry and to love. She was in a country that was eviscerating itself like the pelican mother on Mount Zion in the room of the Last Supper (whether or not there really had been a Last Supper and whether or not this was where it took place, the paradigm remained valid).

And yet. And yet. That shade in Gethsemane by the oil-press. Did I dream him up, out of longing? Am I as much of an innocent as Thomas on his pilgrimage into history, after the tormented William?

Daisy looked around for Gideon. Perhaps he had not followed her in. Which was real: the loving sacrifice on the cross or the threat of the assault rifle? Love abides, Madame Muna had said. There was Rabbi Solomon's faith, pinned so strong, an instinct so simple it would be like breathing. And then the Palestinian in the back of the truck and his eyes that said, this is what we do to each other, see my blind brother beside me, and my sister, Eve, in the box-car.

A priest jostled Daisy. He was trying to sell her a candle while an Israeli woman guiding Germans was speaking, like a keeper in a zoo, of the alleged birth of a child and the year of Common Era.

O, come ye, O, come ye, to Bethlehem.

The green line. The West Bank. All those invisible lines: territorial demarcations, lines ever-shifting between faith and non-faith and wrong faith, past and present, fantasy and the impossibility of truth. Childhood comfort and joy at the Christmas crib in an English country church. Chestnuts and oranges and big cousin Barbara looking after orphan Daisy. Little Lord Jesus laid down his sweet head in the straw in a manger, small and deep below the soaring vaulted arches, like great forest rides, of an English cathedral. And those voices, the singing of boys, the fantasy of innocence.

Daisy emerged from the claustrophobic Grotto. The priest was waiting for her – or perhaps it was another priest.

There was no sign of Gideon. But one of the burly priests, wearing the tall cope of the Eastern Church, was attempting

119

to drive out a small, familiar figure. He looked like a woman shooing a hen with her skirts.

'Jibreel? Whatever are you doing here?'

'Hello, lady.'

Jibreel hopped away gleefully. Daisy shook off both his tormentor and the priest with bad breath and candles for sale, and followed the darting figure through the side door of the Basilica and out, away from the awful huddled shadows and Germans and guides, into the light. Dazzled, she tripped and fell into Gideon's arms.

Kalfayan was not the only person intimate with the underground workings below Old Jerusalem. Eugenia did not even need a map. She had simply been born, so far as she could tell, with a detailed chart already in her head.

So she needed only to close her eyes and look inward to know that where Fedor and the workmen had broken through, there would be – as was revealed – a cave that would serve excellently as an air-raid shelter.

What she did not say, as she supervised the fitting of a small steel door, was that Hezekiah's men, enlarging King David's work, had tunnelled through to another cave below what was now the Holy Sepulchre.

The map in her head reminded her of the arteries of the body which were a very picture of the rivers of the earth, according to Leonardo, that clever old faggot. A lot of rubbish he scribbled, against mule bells and eating the ox and the beating of beds. But he had understood eternity.

Which reminded her, she had felt tired lately and a little cold in her extremities, particularly the feet.

Eugenia climbed the steps to her sunny morning kitchen, Miss Mary's cat at her heels, sat down, thankful to catch her breath, and thought, I should be grateful to go. Finally to end these wanderings. I've dreamed of that often, imagined a return to my father's pool and the golden fish and then either darkness or a great consuming, digesting radiance. But there is Fedor, look, and the love between us: a third party more precious than any child we might have made had our paths crossed long ago.

120

I could not bear to leave. Leave him behind.

'Eugenia, my darling, are you all right?'

'Perfectly, thank you. This cat needs feeding and where are my spectacles?'

'Round your neck.'

'Ah. Of course. I don't want that cat eating the carp.'

'I'd say it's more likely to be the other way round. Is there anything new about Miss Mary in the paper?'

'Cobbler's wife in hiding. A small paragraph. They'll be trying to hush it up.' Eugenia snorted. 'The Peace Conference has been abandoned. That is, it is suspended pending further tripartite talks about talks.'

Fedor was making Eugenia's favourite mid-morning drink: Ovaltine spliced with vodka and a pinch of cinnamon. He put down a saucer of milk for Miss Mary's cat.

'Anything about the air-raid warning?'

'Authorities deny all knowledge. Palestinian plot suspected. Ringleaders arrested. US protests. Peace talks in danger. Temple Mount closed to all but Israeli Arabs. Syria advances on Golan. Punitive raid on Lebanon. Settlers refuse to budge. Escalation of tension predicted for last day of Succot. Accidental shooting of students at Rashidiya High School riot. Bethlehem University closed.' Eugenia sighed. 'Really, I can't think why they ever bother to open.'

Fedor shuddered. 'Oh dear. Hamil says the Armenian's behind it all. He's been distributing leaflets as from the Temple Mount Faithful. Threatening to blow up the El-Aqsa mosque as a preliminary to laying the corner-stone for the new Temple. Again. I think he's having a breakdown.'

'The Armenian?'

'No. Hamil.' Fedor took out one of his thin black cigars but paused in lighting it. 'Hasn't Miss Herbert gone to Bethlehem? Will she be all right?'

'She is a grown-up young woman entirely capable of looking after herself. Striking rather than pretty. She has an interesting pointy nose which compensates for that thin skin. She wears freckles very well.' As she talked Eugenia went on reading. 'Ah, that's better. I do enjoy the small ads. Anonymous discreet lady offers astrological services. Next week Dr Menashe Grossman delivers a lecture at the Beit Shmuel Education Centre: Irony, Judaism and the Jewish Joke. Anglo-Saxon Orthopedic Supplies offer Immediate Relief with Linear Gravity Pillows and Ankle Weights. More astrological services: You, Your Stars and Destiny. Well, one has to remember, Joseph read Pharaoh's dreams and he got to the top. And the Millenium is coming up. One must expect magic.'

Eugenia looked over her spectacles.

'Cheer up, Fedor, dear. It's not the end of the world.'

'Isn't it?'

Emerging into the calm forecourt of St Catherine's Church, Daisy thought how, in this nervy land, peace kept taking her by surprise. She took in the cloisters, the mild sun, the statue, and only then realised that she was still clasped in Gideon's arms. Her body was enjoying the sensation and would have stayed but she stepped back. Her intelligence said: this is not your place.

'I'm sorry. Can we sit down? I lost you.'

'I'm afraid I have to get back soon. I should have said.'

Daisy remembered Gideon at Bethany. In Israel everyone is a soldier. Her view of him had changed since then, but the fact remained: he was a warrior.

'You're not a security policeman, are you?'

Gideon laughed. 'No, I'm not. Nor do I club Palestinians to death.'

The sun was higher in the sky now. Daisy blinked. When she opened her eyes she saw the nuns from Madame Muna's crossing the courtyard, in the shadowed section. Butterflies, she decided. Cabbage whites.

Jibreel had disappeared. She had found Gideon again but where was Thomas? And what was Jibreel doing in Bethlehem and had that been Morgan in the cream convertible?

'Paths cross in mad pursuit,' she said. For just one second, where the nuns had been, she thought she saw Jibreel holding the hand of a woman in blue. A trick of the light.

'Who's that? The statue?'

122

'Saint Jerome. He translated the Bible into Latin. He didn't like pilgrims.'

Daisy thought how he would be in bed. Good. Assertive. She tried not to think of bed.

'You said you were secular. Does that mean you don't believe?'

An ample man, he would be, with age.

'Oh, no. I believe. But I don't practise. I wait for the Messiah time, which means that I abhor fanatics and most politicians. Politicians killed my father. I fight for the Land but I'd give land for peace.'

A pigeon had settled on the head of Saint Jerome.

Daisy said: 'Don't worry. I can hitch a lift back. There's always the nuns. That poetry was wonderful. I liked Halevi. It's queer. It's sacred and sexy at the same time. And that one about Yom Kippur.'

'Oh, yes, Yehuda Amichai. "I stood, for some time in the alcove of an Arab's shop, not far from the Damascus Gate . . . I told him in my heart that my father, too, had such a shop of threads and buttons."'

'More or less what your grandfather said. We are more alike than we are different. Though sometimes that's hard to believe. Is that Morgan Pooley over there? Why is he lurking?' Daisy said quickly, in one breath, before she could change her mind: 'I think you had better go. It wouldn't be a good idea.'

Both knew what she meant.

'Why not?'

She shook her head, once, twice, thrice.

'I'm English. I hate it sometimes but that's what I am. I'm not of your tribe.' She felt an idiot. 'I'm squeamish about Kalashnikov assault rifles and Uzi sub-machine guns.'

'So am I. Will you come with me to Jericho?'

'That is a very corny suggestion,' Daisy said. 'Anyhow, I thought travel had been restricted for tourists?'

Daisy pretended not to notice that Gideon had taken her hand in his and was holding it as though it were a priceless glove, turning it over, running his finger along the palm.

'You have such thin skin.' Reluctantly he gave her back her hand. 'Not for Israelis. I would be responsible for you.'

'I am responsible for myself,' Daisy said. Among the younger Israeli men she had noticed a macho swank. Even Gideon was not entirely free of it. But his eyes were so very blue. And he wooed her with Jericho and poetry.

Just as Gideon bent to kiss her and all would have been lost or won, the nuns flew back across the courtyard, startling the pigeon from the head of the saint. And Morgan Pooley said: 'I say, there you are. How jolly.'

So it was that Daisy walked with Morgan Pooley in Shepherds' Field and Gideon went off in a sulk.

'I'm afraid I'm behaving rather badly. I'm running away from the nuns. That's quite a view, isn't it.'

'Yes.' Daisy smiled. She did like Morgan immensely. 'I mean, yes it's a wonderful view. But what are you doing in Bethlehem, Morgan?'

'Getting away from the tomb row. You know, Sepulchre versus Garden Tomb. The fish thing. The Israeli department of antiquities have put their oar in now. A meeting was called for this morning of all parties, which means a shouting match. I'm beginning to wish they'd never found that fish. And, don't tell the Bish but I must admit I was keeping an eye open for the Virgin. Manifestations are a sort of hobby of mine. Not a squeak though.'

Part-way back in the cream convertible they drew into the side of the road to eat an orange and to appreciate another view, across the falling hills to Jerusalem. Morgan peeled and sectioned Daisy's orange.

'Well, was Bethlehem better?' he asked.

'Yes. No. The Barluzzi wasn't as boring as usual. Quite good, really. But it's creepy, isn't it, the town all closed-up? And I kept thinking I ought to feel something. Well, I did. But to feel *more*. I was expecting too much. Everything.'

Morgan nodded. 'Pilgrim fever. Everyone gets it. The dreary facts are that Augustus may never have called a census. The whole thing could have been cooked up by the chroniclers to fit the birth of the Messiah foretold in Isaiah.'

'So how do you go on believing?'

'I think they call it a leap of faith.' Morgan collected together the parings, wrapped them in a tissue and put them in the glove compartment.

A melodramatic thundercloud had gathered over Jerusalem, although in the Judean hills the sky was still pure and cotton blue.

Daisy said: 'Do you know a boy called Jibreel?'

'Yes. An orphan. Cheeky little monkey. He'll get into trouble one day. Well, we'd better get down before the sky falls. I do hope Gideon Solomon was not upset. These Israelis are so touchy. They think all the English are in love with the Arabs.'

As they took the road again a battered Citroën tried to pass them. And they overtook easily a lorry loaded with nuns and vegetables.

'I forgot to say,' Morgan said as they ripped away from the swaying lorry, 'I called for you at Madame Muna's. There was a message for you.'

'What message?'

'Fedor didn't say. Can't have been important. Oh dear, here it comes. And I'm not absolutely sure I can get the hood up. You wouldn't have an umbrella?'

'A what? Oh. No.'

A furious sky was punishing Jerusalem but Daisy was hardly aware of the premonitory drops as they left the hills and entered the industrial outskirts.

Her fox hair was plastered to her head. But she was thinking of poetry and buttons and threads.

Threads and buttons, thought Daisy.

And while Jibreel the Palestinian orphan teased the snipers on the police-station roof in Manger Square, the woman in blue sat in the small yard beneath the olive tree where the hens ran around, and, remembering that she was a good seamstress, showed the cobbler's wife how to sew on a button without needle or thread.

TWELVE

'That's not a baby. It's a gun,' Barbara said when the girl dropped the shawl and jumped screaming into the aisle. 'Actually, it's a sub-machine gun and are those grenades round her waist?'

It was true about terror. Teddy's mouth was so dry he found it hard to speak.

'I think we're being hijacked,' he said.

The girl had Arab colouring. She seemed unable to stay in one place. Or perhaps this was strategy. She danced as though on coals, waving her rifle and continuing to scream. The potato-faced stewardess who had boarded the plane at Crjzbc backed away in the direction of the cockpit but the girl waved the rifle under her nose.

'What we have to do,' Barbara said, 'is to make ourselves inconspicuous. I've read about it. On no account meet her eye. Do not indulge in heroics and speak very quietly without moving your lips. Her apparent frenzy is a well-known terrorist technique.'

The girl yelled at Barbara, probably in Arabic. She meant, shut up.

Still waving her weapon and clutching the stewardess, the girl backed up the aisle and planted herself in the galley. The stewardess was released and disappeared, returning with the pilot or co-pilot, a tired-looking man in an ill-fitting grey uniform. There was more screeching, in response to which the uniformed one scratched his chin, belched, shrugged and finally led the girl away, presumably into the cockpit.

The passengers who, with the exception of Barbara, had been frozen in shocked silence, stirred and a few exchanged cautious murmurs. The aircraft was so small, they could

126

hear the girl screeching in the cockpit. There was a nervous laugh, a sob. A child whined. An elderly Jew looked as if he were saying a prayer. The sullen stewardess came round collecting passports.

Teddy whispered: 'Why is she doing that?'

'They usually execute Jews first, then Americans.'

'And then?'

'Us. The Brits, that is. Only there aren't any Americans and we are the only British.'

'Ah.'

'Only, of course, she can't shoot anyone in the air. Unless it's a suicide mission.'

Teddy nodded. He was mildly surprised at his own reaction to the drama. A man of so many small fears, he was less frightened than he would have expected had he known this was going to happen.

It couldn't be courage, so perhaps it was adrenalin, but his fish-bowl head had cleared and he had a weird sense of lightness, as if responsibility for his own trivial cares had been lifted from him. For the first time he almost understood the point of Tom's harebrained adventure.

All the same, the immediacies of the present crisis were, quite plainly, terrifying. A few moments ago, the plane had banked and turned. The sun was at a different angle. They must be heading south. There, below, was desert: the first he had ever seen. It was amazingly beautiful: wave upon wave of sand, curled and whorled and heaped and blown, beach upon beach of pure rosy emptiness. And there, what might be a small track of man or a trick of the light.

Then the whining child began to bawl. The stewardess, presumably under orders, reached across and pulled down the window-shutter, so that everything was dim. No one dared to switch on the reading lights.

Teddy thought of Icarus and his fall. He found himself amazingly grateful for the company of Barbara and the sound of her voice.

'Would you mind terribly if I held your hand?' she said.

'Of course not.'

The screeching had stopped. The only sounds now were of the engines and of a child crying in the dark.

Thomas came to his senses only to discover that his eyes were blindfolded, his hands tied, his mouth gagged, so he could neither call out nor see where he was. His head hurt and he lost consciousness again. Then he could see, after all. Perhaps it had been night when he thought he was blind. Now he was aware of a ray of light. He blinked, struggled and failed to free his hands, and by this narrow beam began to make out the shape and nature of his prison.

He was in a cave. There was a small flight of rough steps leading to a door. Undoubtedly locked. Such light as there was came from a cleft in the rock above his head. In the wall there was something that might have been a crudely carved prie-dieu and on the rock surface some roughly hewn graffiti he could not make out.

It was extraordinarily difficult to stand with your hands tied behind you. He gave up the effort, panting and dizzy. Just as he sank to the ground again, he heard a sound like the sky cracking. It might have been a bomb, thunder or an earthquake.

Terror, thirst and the pain at the back of his skull kept Thomas awake for a while. The muffled explosion was repeated several times.

He must have fallen asleep at last because he woke knowing that he had dreamed, though of what he could not remember, except that it was very beautiful and filled with light.

On this, the last, joyous, celebratory day of Succot, the great thunderstorm broke on the heads of schoolchildren marching, gas-masks over their shoulders; on the traffic jam that circled the Old City, the men with sidelocks moaning at the Wailing Wall and the women on the platform overlooking it, setting out the happy picnic for the evening, when families and friends would come together and lovers meet.

The sky cracked and the rain fell on the two thousand armed police patrolling within the City walls. As Israel's enemies mobilised there was a feeling in Jerusalem of both tension and abandon. Israeli Arabs called their children in.

It was an extraordinary, inflammatory amount of love and hatred and passion, loss and longing, to be confined within so few square miles of history, superstition and faith, and all beneath a low, black sky, a dangerous, bruise-coloured purple behind Omar's golden dome.

As the lightning flashed, Magdalena covered the mynah bird's cage with a fringed cloth and went to fetch in the washing. It must have been the weather. She had had a dream that afternoon of a white angel and an empty tomb. And a man who had made her laugh and given her courage: a husband perhaps? A brother? She had woken, weeping.

There were those who were of the flesh and those who were of the spirit.

In the flesh, Eugenia lay with Fedor beneath Miss Mary's magic quilt. The storm had given them both the same headache. They had slept heavily, their dreams entwined, and Fedor had woken afraid.

'Pass me my teeth, Fedor. That was a good dream but you look upset?'

'Just the weather. If only it would rain.'

Eugenia nodded.

'Nothing worse than a dry storm. Shall I tell you a story?'

'Shouldn't we be getting dinner ready? The nuns will be wet.'

But Eugenia knew what was worrying Fedor. It had worried her too, but she had thought about it.

'There is a Christian legend,' she said, 'that beneath Calvary there is a crack in the rock. And when Christ was crucified, his blood ran down through that cleft and splashed on Adam's skull, thus giving him life.'

Fedor looked doubtful. He felt a little sick.

'Do you believe that?'

'Not necessarily. But it makes a good point about the nature of time. It is neither a river nor a road. The worst that we fear, that Jerusalem may fall, that we might be parted, could already have happened. Equally, we may not be at the end but the beginning.'

Fedor was not entirely convinced. If there were no such thing as linear time, why were they both getting older? Why was he afflicted by thinning hair and Eugenia by cold feet?

All the same, he was consoled at a level more vital perhaps, than intellect. Since that first meeting with Eugenia in Cairo he had grown acquainted with miracles. So he might still hope for eternal love and blessed consummation.

And it had started raining. With the easing of the sky, Fedor felt better. Standing at the window, he saw the rain slash down, the heap of dark clouds to the north and, just appearing between their heads and the black sky, a finger of pure gold. His spirit lifted. Maybe it was the ozone in the air but he had a charge of energy. Tomorrow he would be meeting Solly and Hamil at Magdalena's. He would work harder and learn how to play chess. He would go on with his story. He would insist that Solly finally revealed to them the Byzantine ploy. He would touch his toes without fail every morning and night.

He might even remember who he was.

But although he had cheered up, Fedor, laying the tables for dinner, remained confused. If Eugenia were right, the Apocalypse might already have happened and they could be in a new age. If so, it seemed very much like the old one.

Of those of the spirit, there was one who flitted in and out of the flesh. Sometimes he took the form of a Palestinian orphan, sometimes that of a Jew, also of an Arab gardener.

In company with the Messiah who wore the skull-cap, he wandered among the celebrants who were laying out their feast. There was smoked fish and whisky. The rain had stopped and the great party was saved.

Since they had the freedom of time they could see more. The Messiah in the skull-cap pointed to the other celebrants who danced by the light of golden, multi-branched menorah lamps. The dancing men carried torches and there was singing with the dancing: a joyous shout of psalms.

'Do you remember?' said the fat Messiah.

'Oh yes. What a party that was.'

The fat Messiah drew his hand across his eyes as

they watched the spirits dancing, whirling, singing, torch-throwing. His foot tapped. He began to clap.

'I am not weeping,' he said. 'I am laughing.'

'I say, I didn't interrupt anything, did I?' Morgan said.

It was dark already by the time they got stuck in yet another traffic jam, a couple of miles from the Jaffa Gate. At least it had stopped raining.

For a moment Daisy could not think what he was talking about.

'Oh, you mean with Gideon? No, not at all. That is to say, I was quite relieved to see you.' She pulled her fingers through her wet hair. It would dry in awful tight curls. 'You saved me from complications.'

Coming the other way, on the empty side of the road, several security police-vans yipped past followed by a more military-looking vehicle.

'I wonder what's going on,' Morgan said. He pulled a face. 'You know the Israelis invented the Uzi sub-machine gun? I'd have thought a good many women wouldn't mind complications with Gideon Solomon.'

'Maybe.'

It was easier to say difficult things after dark, Morgan thought.

He said quickly, before he could regret it: 'I've been thinking about you rather a lot. I'd have said I was in love with you if I knew what love was. I do in my head. It's just that I haven't much experience of the flesh. In fact, not any. So what do you think?'

Daisy was startled. Then she said carefully: 'Morgan, I like you more than almost anyone I know. But I've got a feeling that a lot of people fall for the idea of being in love. It's a very strong urge, like wanting to believe, wishing for faith. What I mean is, do you think that might have happened to you? The wanting?'

'Actually, you might well be right.' Morgan was first downcast then very slightly relieved. Or, he knew he would be relieved, later. At the moment he was a little disappointed. 'I hope you don't mind.'

Daisy kissed him on the cheek. 'I'm honoured. I'll always care about you.'

Morgan blew his nose. They sat for a while. He said: 'Did you know the Song of Songs was taken from an Arab love poem?'

'No, I didn't. Morgan, tell me, what do you really feel about the tomb? This row's upset you, hasn't it? It matters to you.'

They had begun to move again. Morgan made his confession lightly.

'I'll tell you something. I've got a fantasy that one day we'll find three words in the Garden Tomb. *Hic Jacet Cristus*. Not a prayer, I know. I've never said this to anyone else.'

'Perhaps you will. I hope so. Truly.'

When they arrived at Madame Muna's, Daisy asked Morgan in.

'Thanks. But I'd better get back. It was naughty of me to skip the meeting but I do hate shouting. You've no idea how aggressive the Eastern churches are. If only we were RC. They're pretty good in a fight. Maybe I'll call in later?'

'Yes. Do that. And thank you.'

The dim lobby was full of nuns in a state of excitement and exhaustion. They were in a mood approaching hysteria and at the same time plucking parts of vegetables from their soaking clothes. Behind the counter Fedor was cowering before the formidable Mother Matthew.

'And you did not say we would have to travel back with vegetables. I shall wish to speak to Madame Muna,' she concluded.

As the nuns made their way upstairs, leaving behind them a trail of wet footprints and a quantity of lettuce leaves, Fedor groaned and clutched his head. When he passed Daisy her key, his hand was shaking. He looked even thinner, and shorter.

'Fedor, what's going on?'

'Oh dear, everything, Miss Herbert. The Little Sisters of Sorrow were not at all happy in the vegetable lorry. And it appears that Sister Angelica has disappeared. Bolted, I'd say, and who can blame her? And now they've blown up the Grotto of the Nativity.'

'The nuns have blown up the Grotto?'

'No, no. And fortunately no one was hurt. No one was caught either but they've arrested twenty students from Bethlehem University. It's a bit of a hotbed, you know, but they can't close it completely because it was set up by Vatican decree.' Fedor chewed on his black cigar. 'These poor people,' he said, his face creased with worry.

Daisy saw the face of the Arab in the back of the police-van: look, this is how it is, how I am.

'You mean the Arabs?'

Fedor shook his head.

'All of them. I know nothing of politics but I am so sorry for them, these Arabs and Jews, all people who have nowhere to live. I feel this so much perhaps because I think I once had a home and lost it. And the children on both sides. They are born to hate, that is how they grow up.'

Daisy nodded. 'But you have a home now, Fedor.'

'Oh, yes. Wherever Eugenia is, that is my home.' He looked gratefully at Daisy. 'And you were not caught in the trouble in Bethlehem. We are thankful for that.'

Daisy was just turning away when she remembered.

'Fedor, have you seen Thomas Curtis?'

'Not today at all, I'm afraid. In fact, when I went to make his bed it had not been slept in.'

'That's odd. Well, I expect he'll turn up.'

Fedor threw up his hands.

'And I nearly forgot! There is a telegram for you. Here, in your cubbyhole.'

'A telegram? How strange. I thought they'd abolished them.'

'It is not from England.'

'Thanks, Fedor.'

Daisy wanted to get to her room to dry her hair. She wanted, most of all, to find Thomas, but the telegram intrigued her. She sat down by a dusty yucca to read it in the lobby.

'Oh dear,' she said.

'Not bad news, I hope?'

'Well, not really. Just a bit. It seems to be from my cousin and I think she's coming to Jerusalem. But it doesn't make much sense. Look, Fedor.'

The telegram read: COMINKJOINSUNNEST ZTOP BERBERA ZTOP CRJZBC ZTOP.

'The message is more or less clear,' Daisy said. 'But where is she. Where has it come from?'

'Crjzbc,' Fedor said.

'What did you say?'

'The second word from the end. That's the place.'

'However do you know?'

'I don't know.'

Although the storm had cleared the weather remained heavy over Jerusalem. The last evening of Succot was celebrated without rain or air raid or unusual disturbance.

There were, however, a number of people with headaches.

Thomas's went right round his skull and half-way down his spine. A thug in a kiffiyeh had come and left him a wodge of pitta bread and a few unpleasant-looking beans. Black and acid to the tongue. When Thomas tried to question him he got his face slapped, hard.

He should have been in despair and for a while he was. Then words came into his head as clearly as if they had been spoken.

> Lost to be found.
> Resurrect in my own life.

He thought, I have broken. My mind has gone already. He heard himself say: 'William?' And then: 'My Lord?'

Morgan's headache was so frightful he was beyond consolation, even from the little cat Sheba, the one piece of flesh upon this earth that he knew he loved.

He would never have found out if he hadn't gone into the garden, looking for Sheba. And as he called her name and then, puss, puss, puss, realised from the sight of the trampled fig, weeping its milk upon the earth, that there was something terribly wrong. That he had failed even in his modest role as guardian.

134

Morgan put his face under the cold tap. Then he thought of the telephone calls he must make, the thunderbolts that would fall on his head, picked up the bottle of Celebration Cream, put it down and poured himself a large whisky, the malt Mrs Bish had given him the Christmas before last.

Then he decided to make another call first. But just as he was about to dial Madame Muna's, the telephone rang.

'Morgan?'

'Daisy. I was just going to call you.'

'Listen, Morgan, I've had a telegram from Barbara. She's coming to Jerusalem. I was supposed to have told you that she's after you for that book. Why were you ringing me? You can't come round?'

'No. Something awful's happened. The tomb has been vandalised. The fish. They must have used a pick-axe. It's broken, mostly gone. And there's been another landslide.'

'How terrible. Can I help? Shall I come over?'

'Thanks. But there's not much you could do, or anyone. I suppose I'll get the sack. Maybe see you tomorrow. I'll have to make some calls.'

Alone, truly, terribly alone, Morgan did the telephoning that had to be done, then he made scrambled egg, couldn't eat it and put it on the floor for Sheba, and went down into the garden.

There were few stars but the moon at last appeared, only just on the wane, bright enough to read the words on the stone he knew by heart: 'Now in the place where he was crucified there was a garden; and in the garden a new sepulchre, wherein was never man yet laid.'

At that same moment the sky cleared over Bethlehem, clouds were swept away, a fresh wind came up and the sky was full of stars.

The woman in blue, Miss Mary, said: 'Look!'

They tipped their faces, like moon-flowers, to the sky. Then Mary gasped and smiled and touched her belly. And the cobbler's wife put a hand there, too, to feel in wonder where a new life turned and quickened.

'How long to your time?' she said.

THIRTEEN

*T*eddy wondered how he could be tormented by thirst and at the same time need so desperately to pee. He dared not ask, for that would be calling attention to himself.

Survivors of similar situations had talked about the usefulness of poetry. The hostage who had no inner life was lost. So many words Teddy thought he knew but none would come to him now. 'The long habit of living indisposeth us for dying': Thomas Browne, of course, but what use was someone else's stoicism? Teddy felt not at all disposed for dying. In fact, strangely, through this long, wearisome and dangerous journey there had grown in him as in a fledgling bird learning the purpose of its wings, an appetite for living, for life.

No, don't think about wings just now.

Barbara had murmured to him that she had the same problem. Teddy looked at her now. She was sitting, eyes closed in concentration, silently moving her lips in accord with some inner voice.

Teddy whispered: 'What are you thinking about?'

'I'm making lists.'

'What lists?'

'You don't want to know.'

'I do.'

'It's a grocery list. I do it every Sunday.'

'That doesn't matter.'

'All right. Quarter Twining's Earl Grey tea, half a pound Patna rice, one Lurpak butter, one Flora Light, two Wisk, one Stergene, one Gold Blend Nescafé.' Barbara opened one eye. 'You can't possibly be interested?'

'I am.'

'OK. One frozen vegetable lasagne, one frozen Cod Mornay, six free-range eggs, two tins red kidney beans, one packet Epicure pitted prunes, one packet Oat Bran Flakes.'

'Are you a vegetarian?'

'No. I get my meat at Sainsbury's.'

'This is terribly interesting. I like cooking. Do you have a microwave?'

Barbara opened both eyes wide and looked at Teddy as though he were mad.

The girl had emerged from the cockpit and was ranging down the aisle again. She stopped to scream at Barbara and Teddy.

'American?'

It was the first time Teddy had seen Barbara lost for words.

'No.'

'German?'

Teddy shook his head again. 'No.'

'Jews?'

'No.'

It was a perilous moment. It passed through Teddy's mind that the instinct to survival was very selfish. In an extremity that he could for the first time in his life visualise, man will eat human flesh. He felt certain that there was not one passenger in this plane who was not praying: take him, oh Lord, not me. And in that same second he was blessed by an intuitive hunch that the girl was the one who was truly alone and the most desperately frightened of them all.

She was biting on a grenade pin. No one spoke. No one moved. Even the bawling child had been somehow silenced.

Barbara was frozen in her seat. Now, for all these human souls in their terribly fragile airborne prison, this could be the time to give up the long habit of living.

Teddy leaned across Barbara and addressed the girl: 'Don't be afraid,' he said, 'you have nothing to fear.'

That morning an Arab youth had been found crucified near Ramallah. A mile away, a West Bank Israeli settler had died from gunshot wounds. Cars had been torched on the way to Jerusalem airport.

The American Secretary of State swam his regular ten lengths in the pool of the King David Hotel. Alongside him swam his opposite number. It was six a.m.

Back in the Secretary's suite they took breakfast without their advisers. That is, the Secretary ate toast, muesli and fruit and drank coffee while his opposite number tucked into the usual gigantic Israeli breakfast.

The Secretary winced. He had long ago decided that the first requirement for any would-be negotiator in this part of the world was a gut of iron.

'See here, Dan, it's difficult for you, it's difficult for us. You've got a Palestinian state already in the Gaza strip. Hand it over to Egypt and you win every way. Give Cairo the headache and get world opinion off your back. That's my last offer this time round. And if you don't pull back those settlers on the West Bank the whole country's going to blow up in your face.'

'Homer, you're an old friend, so you know, we look after our own shop. As for the rest, you can say that we are considering the possibility of reducing our nuclear capacity.'

'The one you haven't got any more?'

'That's right. But naturally, only on condition that we have American support in the matter of arms should our present aggressors take the first step. And officially, I am empowered to explain last night's outrage. As you know, the dafawin Arabs of the West Bank despise the Israeli Arabs, who in turn hate the dafawin. The victim was an Israeli Arab. The perpetrators are known to have come from Nablus. But your limousine's waiting.'

The Secretary sighed.

'Right, Dan. Until the next time. I guess we say peace talks not abandoned but stalled.'

'If you'd like to look, the statement's already drafted. Nothing personal, Homer.'

'Nothing personal. The Lord was right, Dan. You're a stiff-necked lot.'

'Shalom, Homer.'
'Shalom, Dan. You're going to need it.'

The Listeners were busier even than usual. The American Secretary of State was low on the list of the priority eavesdropping stations. And while the peculiar horror of the crucifixion was a concern that crossed all boundaries of faith, it was simply one of many affairs requiring monitoring.

From the windowless bunker in West Jerusalem ears were bent to catch whispers from as far away as the Golan Heights and as close as the Holy Sepulchre. Weighed and sifted were rumours from Bethlehem and voices of recrimination within the offices of the Security Police.

Since the crucifixion, the explosion in Bethlehem, the incident at the Garden Tomb and the false-alarm air raid, the voices had risen to a clamour: the cries of left-wingers, right-wingers, Jews, Arabs, Christians, peaceniks, settlers, Syrians, orthodox extremists – the Listeners heard them all but did not judge for that was not their job.

They were faintly puzzled by a new voice from the area of the Holy Sepulchre but well below ground. It sounded like a man singing, a Christian hymn.

But they had listened for so long, they had almost forgotten why they were listening or what they were listening for.

Perhaps one day they would succeed in bugging the Armenian.

Or, in her death-pangs, Jerusalem herself might speak. If she did, that would be the last cry ever heard by the Collectors of Voices.

Since the new night-curfew restrictions imposed on both West and East Jerusalem and the indefinite closing of the Temple Mount area, by late evening, when Fedor made his way to Magdalena's, the streets of the Old City were almost empty. Jews were sleeping off Succot parties or extending the holiday elsewhere. The Israeli Arabs were keeping to their homes, the few tourists to their hotels.

Finding himself unusually nervous in the streets and alleys

he knew so well, Fedor trotted faster than usual and took the long way round, avoiding the Via Dolorosa.

He carried his gas-mask and hoped not to run into a police patrol. Not that anyone would be interested in him but the fact remained that, lacking nationality, date or place of birth, his identity papers were less than adequate. And there was, probably in his imagination only, something following about the shadows.

Eugenia always said: when afraid think of something quite different. So Fedor, trying to run fast but not too fast, worried about the nice English girl Eugenia seemed to like, and how she had appeared upset, first by the telegram from Crjzbc and then by the fact that the Englishman Thomas Curtis had either disappeared or left without paying his bill.

This morning Miss Herbert looked as though she had slept badly. Fedor guessed that Berbera in Crjzbc was the person she was hoping would not come. But she seemed even more concerned about the Englishman who kept knocking things over and barking his shins.

When Fedor told Eugenia she said quite firmly: 'Give her the pass-key to his room.'

Miss Herbert had stayed in the room for several hours. At midday Fedor had taken her a sandwich and found her sitting on the unslept-in bed, reading a book.

'Not our business,' Eugenia said. But she looked pleased.

'My darling,' Fedor said, 'you are not by any chance making matches?'

Eugenia smiled. She was in a quite exceptionally good mood.

'Certainly not,' she said. 'Matches make themselves or they are not worth making.' She had slept late and was propped up on top of Miss Mary's quilt, drinking something from a tooth-mug and knitting wildly. Her feet were bare. 'Surely you remember Cairo?'

'Of course,' Fedor answered.

Tenderly, he knelt beside the bed and kissed that beloved instep. Eugenia had bunions from wearing shoes too tight for ever. But Fedor did not see them, only that captive curve.

140

Eugenia said: 'You know I am a profoundly selfish woman?'

'Oh yes, my heart, I know.'

'So you must be the most selfless man on earth.'

'Almost. Not quite.'

As Fedor cradled the precious arch, Miss Mary's magic quilt was suddenly changed. Screeching peacock and dumb flamingo were gone and in their place there was a pattern of flowers and smiles.

'So, the young Englishwoman – do you know what she was reading? If she discovered anything?'

Fedor was enormously relieved to find Solly already there when he arrived at Magdalena's. In the part of his life he remembered the next most precious thing to his love for Eugenia was his friendship with Solly and Hamil.

Answering Solly, he thought how there was something in particular about the rabbi that always cheered him and settled his fears. Perhaps it was his good-humoured bulk. Whatever the reason, in Solly's company Fedor stopped panting and felt safer.

'Yes, I do,' he said, 'and she did.' Fedor paused while Magdalena brought another glass and a large carafe of angels' pee. She smelled even muskier than usual. Was it the weather that had brought out her scent, like a flower's? Fedor blushed. 'Miss Herbert showed me the book. It seems that Thomas Curtis has an ancestor who made a pilgrimage. He had a vision in Jerusalem then he went to Sinai. She's convinced that is where Thomas Curtis has gone and she's going after him. I think she's also running away from someone called Berbera.'

'You mean she's going to Eilat?'

Fedor nodded. 'I told her the road to the airport was dangerous. There might not even be a flight. But she's very strong-headed.'

'Ah, love,' Solly said.

Fedor was startled.

'You think they're in love? That's what Eugenia said. But they hardly know each other.'

'And what does that have to do with anything?' Solly wagged his head. 'And I think my poor grandson is struck too.'

In one of his frequent, ample gestures, more eloquent than words, Solly shrugged deeply and opened his arms wide. As Eugenia always said, these Jews never stopped talking with their mouths and their hands.

A nippy breeze had come up. Solomon and Fedor moved indoors. Magdalena, out of customers of both kinds – drinkers and those who sought her favours upstairs – was leaning on the bar vaguely wiping glasses but really watching an old American Western without the sound. She understood Hebrew but, as she often said, pictures were best then you could make up the story to suit yourself.

'Awk,' said the mynah bird.

'Shut up,' said Magdalena. 'So where's our friend, the imam?'

'Hamil is coming,' Solly said.

And just as though the rabbi had conjured him, there, parting the bead curtain, was the ravaged, wild-eyed figure of the imam, gasping for breath like a man pursued to the edge of hell.

Fedor sighed. He had hoped so much that they could settle tonight into their old ways – chess and the telling of stories.

But one look at Hamil confirmed his worst guess.

The man, his old friend, was either in danger of losing his life. Or out of his mind.

'He is responsible!'

Hamil was so distracted he absently poured himself a glass of angels' pee. Fedor opened his mouth to remind him that he didn't drink and then decided that if Allah was a God worth having he would overlook this minor infringement of the rules.

Instead he asked: 'The Armenian? Responsible for what?'

'Everything! The false air-raid alarm, the Bethlehem Grotto, the Garden Tomb, the crucifixion, the collapse of the peace talks.'

'How do you know?'

'I have been following him everywhere. I would have killed him with my bare hands. But the mukhabarat secret intelligence are following Mossad, who are following me and Kalfayan's men are following the mukhabarat.' Hamil filled his glass again. 'Not here! I came by way of the tunnels. Never would I lead those scorpions here.' He raised his narrow fingers to heaven. 'You are my friends, this is my home.'

The angels' pee must have helped. Hamil was a better colour.

Solomon had been watching Hamil's face but so far said nothing. Now he spoke with gentle firmness.

'Hamil, this is not your home. As my home is with Miriam, Fedor's with Madame Muna, so yours is with Hamida. You are still attached to her, I think?'

The imam nodded. Tears sprang from his eyes.

'Forever.' Now the tears were running down his cheeks. 'If you had known her. She was my pigeon and, after Allah and his Prophet, my love. She was as the virgins who await us in Paradise, bashful, dark eyed, as chaste as the sheltered eggs of ostriches. May Allah, the compassionate, the merciful, forgive me. Perhaps I gave her too much of the love that should have been his. And this is his punishment – that she is turned to a barren screech-owl. I cannot bear to live with her.'

The angels' pee had had an amazing effect on Hamil. He was sobbing openly.

Solly handed him a red-spotted handkerchief.

'My friend, God does not measure love. There can never be too much. There are only two courses open to you. You must put her away or beat her.'

'Beat her?'

'Not too hard. Just a little, preferably on the backside, would be enough. It is permitted in your Book. And when you have beaten her, you must love her well, in bed and out of bed.'

Fedor was so startled he could not speak. Magdalena had given up any pretence of watching television. Instead, all eyes were turned on Hamil.

At last he answered: 'You may be right, Solly. I shall think about it. Perhaps I shall try.'

'Good. Magdalena, bring another carafe and black coffee for the imam.' Solly, who had been looking unusually severe, was once more genial. 'Tonight, no more talk of Armenians or anti-Christs. Hamil, blow your nose and drink your coffee.'

'Are we going to play chess?' Fedor asked.

'No. You will go on with your story. You remember where you had got to?'

'I think so. But what about the Indian defence? The Leningrad game? The Byzantine gambit?'

'Another time. Magdalena, my dear, if you would be kind enough to turn off the lights and bring us a candle? Stories are always better by candle-light.'

Magdalena shrugged her hips.

'OK. If I can listen?'

'Of course.'

So Hamil blew his long nose, nearly extinguishing the candle, Magdalena covered the mynah bird and pulled up a chair, and Solly nodded to Fedor, who began.

'Then he gathered together half a smoked ham and some apples from the cellar. He put on the rough wolf-coat that had once been the farmer's pride, shut his eyes, turned round three times, and set off south, to find his love.'

It was already midnight when Fedor began his story-telling and it would be close to dawn before he finished.

Daisy too, saw dawn come up. She had done her packing, pushing into her flight-bag a clean nightie, her coolest Indian angari trousers and cotton mull top, toothbrush and tooth-paste, Opal Fruit sweets, sun-hat and a tube of sun-block. Where she was going she imagined it would be very hot. Meanwhile for the journey, she would wear jeans, shirt and sweater.

Once packed, she had not been able to sleep. Instead she read again the passage that had most struck her in William Curthose's journal. There was no doubt about it, she felt sure. Thomas had followed William south to Sinai.

Was she following him to avoid Barbara, she wondered? It didn't matter. The urge to go after Thomas on his crazy errand was very strong and very simple.

She thought of Thomas, she thought of William. She had read all day and then reread, very nearly in tears, not so much for William the passionate pilgrim, as for the husband far from home, expecting never to return.

Well, for both of them: for William kneeling in joy in Jerusalem and lost in the desert; and for the William in Thomas.

Daisy drowsed but did not sleep. She continued to read. As Thomas had said, there was very little about William's amazing survival and his return to Jerusalem. Just one page covered the four years before he took ship for Cyprus, Italy, England and Kent. Some pages must have been lost or stolen. This was not an opening but a continuation.

So was I set free and almost at once again Confined. The wind blows hard for Home, I am sick with the groan of the timbers and the stench of this Vessel, which is a very Image of our voyage from the waters of our Birth that we may call Creation to the certain Corruption of our flesh.

Still, even in this cruel mass of green Ocean, reduced as I am to a thing of Bone tossed by the curling seas that heap themselves at my back and may yet swallow me, I can affirm that the Dead must certainly awake. This I assert not only since, with St Paul, I saw our Lord out of his due time; that is a matter of Divinity: He is with us at all times and the fault lies not in His absence but in our Unbelieving that we see Him not each day. I speak not of Visions or Popish Miracles and bleeding Relics, but of His presence in our most ordinary businesses; when we walk in our gardens, tend our orchards; when our grandchildren run to us or we sit quietly in the evening with our wives, there He is, not in narrow Goodness as it is most often perceived but in our apprehension of Happiness, our taking of it and giving it in Love. A man who has the possibility of Joy in the sensible world and shuns it, I count a poor derelict that he sees not Paradise is both in the Celestial sphere and on this earth within us and without.

As for the raising of the Dead, I call not *Lazarus* from *Abraham*'s bosom. For in the desert was I not in company with the Ancients of whom I have written? I saw *Ruth* the Moabite and heard the stutter or impediment of speech of *Moses* himself. These were not Creatures of sand that we call mirages for they touched me and I them and *Naomi* brought me, when I was fainting to death, a bowl of curds and goat's milk. I heard the thunder too, and saw the fearful machines of those of Latter Days who shall live after us.

Should I publish this evidence in my life both Philosophers and Clerics will shout out against me. But this is my certain belief: that Time is not as we imagined to be reckoned by chronometer, but an Element in which the living and the dead may wander freely. So in consigning our remains to ashes or deep grave, those who mourn and perform the obsequies for our ruined flesh and bone, should not weep but know that we stand beside them; that we, who appear to their sad eyes gone away, are folk still upon the earth but with a Wonderful Liberty. Throwing away our time-pieces we may as we choose, stay in the chair by our hearths, attend our own births, ride with *Elijah* in his chariot or watch the children of our great-grandchildren at play in a spring field.

Thus people speak of ghosts and hauntings when all they have seen is one of the multitude who stand and move upon the earth, as I saw, whom *Naomi* took for dead. So the Lord I witnessed was a young man and weary already of what would come to Him. Born, He was already Crucified.

I ask my widow, if the promised storm should swallow me but leave these words, that they be not published with my first writings on this Peregrination, for they would be taken for madness. I believe that in the desert I died, in the ordinary sense, and perhaps again in my confinement in Jerusalem; but through this dying was granted a rare sight of Eternity. It is against all Reason and accordingly against the spirit of our times. Yet I take Reason to be the poorest of all Measures, a mark of the poverty of spirit we wear as if we were delivered by the good midwife, wrapped, even at our first lusty cry, in our winding-sheets.

But I am still a man, aware of but unpractised in the Adorable Infinity of which I write. I put down these words in a small cabin on a craft that appeared in harbour as a figment of my Deliverance and is now so small, shuddering and straining in that undersea turmoil that heralds a tempest. The people are Moorish and as like to cut my throat and the Captain's as they are to deliver us safe.

From my cot there is no thing still or certain in this world. A following sea both pushes us home and threatens to break us. I swear this is a wilderness more terrible even than the desert. My words make rubbish before my eyes, like the ashes of the dead whipped by a wind from Hell. We are such Pygmies. We run under bare poles.

Daisy read and slept and read and then could read no more. She thought of Thomas reading this and wanted to put her arms around him and around William too. The two men shared what she could only think of as a sweetness of soul.

A postcard had fallen from between the pages. She picked it up. How odd. There was something familiar about the postmark. She had heard or read that word before: CRJZBC.

In the bowels of Jerusalem Thomas must have slept because he woke and thought he was dead.

Then he remembered. He was alive, but a prisoner. Or was he? No one had been near him for a night and a day, he had been neither tortured nor even questioned.

When he could get the strength together he would try that door again. Meanwhile, there was still a little water left and a scrap of dry pitta bread. Also a handful of olives that had not been there the night before, along with a memory, or the memory of a dream: something to do with William.

147

He had been sleeping in a foetal position. He sat up and stretched. What an irony, he thought: a cell is what I sought and that is what I have. Now I no longer want it. William came out of the desert white-haired, with a theory about time and eternity and the everlasting vision of a god in a garden.

Perhaps for a while William had been mad. Perhaps in a sense he did lose his life to save it. And those four missing years in Jerusalem? William had written of the desert and the voyage and covered the years between with only a few lines suggesting that he had been taken captive by 'those Turks who by persecution and neglectfulness have made this Queen of Cities a dung-heap.' He mentioned that 'a Rabby' had saved him, a man who 'even of that faith of the Israelites was a Christian trewe in the sense of our Lord's understanding.'

Thomas remembered the words because he had read them so many times, puzzled that William the great complainer had said nothing of the hardships he must have endured, only that: 'They know not what a poor thing they hold in my Body, for my Soul hath the freedom of Eternity.'

Thomas wondered if he himself were going mad. Last night – or was it yesterday? – he had felt William's hand on his shoulder. There had been nothing miraculous about it, simply a certainty that William was with him and now he had gone, leaving behind a handful of olives.

A thin light trickled through the shaft or cleft in the rock above, so it must be day.

William went home to his wife. Thomas was by no means sure of going anywhere ever again. He retched on an empty stomach, felt a little emptier and thought, what a queer thing: he had come to Jerusalem looking for William, careless of his own life; and now, in the strangest of circumstances, had found him. And when it was perfectly possible that he might die, most wanted to live. He thought of Daisy and realised that the first moment he saw her he had not merely fallen in love with her but recognised her, as his home, his place, his wife. He desired her in the simplest of ways with his flesh and at the same time as a country in which he had already travelled, if only he had had the wit to see. If she would open the gate and let him in, the girl of odd courage, fox-hair, thin skin.

But why should she? She had said nothing, done nothing even to imply.

Thomas had cramps in every limb. It was vaguely cheering to remember that William was seasick on the voyage to Cyprus.

Better not think of Daisy. Concentrate. Eat three olives and try to get together the strength to shout, not to flail out against panic.

Words, they cannot help. Even one word. The echo of your own voice.

Nothing came. Empty skull. Afraid.

Have a pee, down there, where the earth slopes into what might be the mouth of a tunnel. Too small for me. Think of England. When I was a child and mother flew away I was lonelier than this.

Thomas watched a small spider most elegantly weaving a web and smiled. In theory, where there is a spider there must be a fly and air and a way in and thus a way out.

The England he chose to remember was not that land of drenched laurels in an Oxford suburban garden nor the close comforts invented by Teddy in Bedford Row, but a land Thomas could barely have known, perhaps had invented or forgotten: a country of meadows and orchards, soft light, sweet voices in churches now empty, gone to dust.

If you can't shout then sing, as you did yesterday; first, uncertainly from a dry throat, then more strongly. Mother on her kind wings, Daisy, William, Teddy – everyone Thomas had loved or half-loved or longed to love – their faces merged and glimmered and teased and tempted and blessed him, and kept him company in one golden suffusion of light, as he sang for comfort and rescue.

The Arab whose family had held the key to the Holy Sepulchre since Saladin, performed the ritual wash, made his first prayers of the day, yawned, scratched, drank his coffee and was on his way to open the first door, in no hurry, when

149

he heard the Sepulchre of the idolatrous Christians sing out
with a powerful voice:

> Love Divine, all loves excelling,
> Joy of Heav'n, to earth come down,
> Fix in us Thy humble dwelling,
> All Thy faithful mercies crown.

FOURTEEN

'Is it raining?' Fedor asked.

'No, but it will be.'

Eugenia was standing at the window wearing, as a dressing-gown, a Kaffe Fassett coat she had knitted through the terrible time of Saddam's air raids. Her choice of colours was idiosyncratic, ranging from her favourite purple to petrol yellow. One side was too short, the other trailed on the ground and since she could not be bothered to sew in the ends the garment was in constant danger of unravelling itself. When Eugenia strode around the house in this amazing concoction of lurid stars Miss Mary's cat would stalk but never dare to catch the trailing hem.

'The forecast was good?'

Fedor wondered how Eugenia always knew what the weather would do: if she had meteorological gifts or a concealed third eye in her forehead through which she could see into the future. But then, he reminded himself, Eugenia's view of time was as personal and unusual as her approach to a knitting pattern.

Fedor had got home just before dawn and showered twice to wash off any traces of Magdalena's musk. All the same, Eugenia had turned in her sleep and snorted.

Now he dressed quickly and followed her down to the morning kitchen. After the bedroom, this was his favourite room and he thought, if there were a paradise, his own chosen heaven might be an eternity here, among Eugenia's herbs and pans and cobwebbed cookery books and Miss Mary's potted geraniums.

Fedor yawned.

'I ought to check the dining-room.'

151

'I looked. It's empty. The nuns won't be down yet. Their clothes are still drying. I heard them sneezing.'

Eugenia was putting on the coffee. She never asked what went on at Magdalena's. She knew that if it were interesting, Fedor would tell.

Something was up this morning. He had already smoked two of his cigars, before breakfast.

'Miss Herbert's flying to Eliat. She'll want her breakfast,' he said, but didn't move.

Eugenia set down two cups of coffee and sat facing him across the table.

'Well?' she said.

'I think I'm beginning to remember. That is, that story I've been telling about the boy, I suddenly thought it could be me. I haven't said anything to Solly or Hamil but the queer thing was, I knew what would happen next without thinking. I knew he would go south to find his love, and he'd swim a river and climb a mountain in the snow. And he'd hide in a freight-car full of cattle – I can still smell them, I didn't mind the smell, I was used to it on the farm, and they were warm.

'And for a while I lived as a beggar and thief. I was hungry. Once I was flogged. That was in an Arab country. Then I lived in the City of the Dead.'

'In Cairo?'

Eugenia reached for the vodka bottle and spliced their coffee.

'Yes. Where the poor make their homes in the tombs of their ancestors. It wasn't as bad as you might think and it was luxury for me. Someone was kind, a woman. And then I worked.'

Abruptly, Fedor gasped and covered his face with his hands. Then, in an unconscious gesture, he wiped the palms on his trousers, wiped and wiped, his face stricken.

'My darling, drink your coffee. Stop. The past is rubbish and may never have happened. I have said before, there is too much remembering.'

'No, I have to.' Shakily, Fedor took a gulp of coffee. 'It was an abattoir. The cries of the animals and the blood. That

152

was a different smell. I worked all hours and even in my sleep I could smell death. It choked me. I could never wash it from my hands. That is not in the story. I haven't told Solly or Hamil. I have left it out so the story is a lie.'

Fedor looked up. Tears were streaming down his face. He wiped his eyes and drank the coffee which was almost entirely vodka, and his hand steadied.

'I should go up to the dining-room.'

'Plenty of time. It will be the midday flight, if there is a flight at all. The next things that happened were better, weren't they?'

'Oh, yes.' Miss Mary's small cat came into the kitchen through the open window. It sniffed the geraniums, plopped to the floor and hooped itself round Fedor's ankle. He smiled. 'I took a job washing up in a small hotel. I was glad of the work and I thought perhaps I could wash away the blood.

'Then I forget. Then I remember. I was a waiter and one of the gigolos broke his leg so I became a partner at the *thés dansants*. The owner's wife gave me an old suit of her husband's. It was so worn I put boot-black on the elbows.

'On my Fridays off I would go to the zoo. I saved my *pourboires* from the European and Levantine women to buy buns to feed the animals in the zoo. By feeding those poor beasts I was honouring the dead of the abattoir.

'And one Friday evening, after the zoo, I was passing a very grand hotel when a *calèche* drew up and I saw first the toe of a golden sandal and in the same second the most beautiful and perfect instep in the whole world.'

Eugenia laughed. 'And I slipped and you caught me, first cradling my foot and then taking my hand. Without you, my darling, I might have broken not just my leg but my neck. But you have forgotten what happened next, haven't you?'

'Yes. But I thought you didn't believe in stories about what happened next?'

'I don't. But I can always make an exception.' Eugenia stood. She kissed the top of Fedor's head, on the bald patch. Her back caught her as it did often nowadays. Age was a strange affliction, she thought, for one who tumbled, as she did, through eternity in an everlasting loop. 'I can

153

hear someone in the dining-room. It's colder, isn't it? I'm cold.'

She counted out the croissants. She filled one coffee pot for Daisy. Although the sun shone brilliantly, the shutters rattled, Miss Mary's cat was nervy. In remembering, would Fedor lose his innocence? 'So that's all?'

Fedor was chewing on a dead cigar.

'No. Almost but not quite.'

'What else?'

'That telegram for Miss Herbert reminded me and I think I know where I came from. It's a small place of no importance called Crjzbc.'

'What did you say?'

'Crjzbc.'

Daisy stood at the gate to Madame Muna's in the sunshine, looking for a cab.

Barbara woke, groggy, in a large room. She was in one of two twin beds. There was a man in the other. A palm waved outside the window. There was a television set, along with two comfortable-looking chairs and two sets of luggage side by side. The man in the other bed turned over, groaned and opened his eyes. It was Teddy Short.

Barbara heard herself say: 'Where are we?'

'Surely you remember?' Teddy said. 'The Holiday International Hotel, Aqaba. Nothing to do with the crazy girl. After all that, it turned out that we had engine trouble and Moscow airport was closed – another coup perhaps. So we landed here anyway, which is where she wanted to go.'

Now it came back to Barbara. On first waking she had imagined that the whole terrifying business had been a nightmare. But she had been in a plane that was hijacked. She had been dumped with the other passengers at some primitive airport in a desert, waited hours for transport, answered a lot of foolish questions put to her by incompetent officials, been strip-searched most humiliatingly by a half-veiled woman.

Which reminded her. She glanced down and was thankful to find that she must have gone to bed half-dressed: she was still wearing her cardigan.

154

'Where's Aqaba?'

Teddy had undressed. He was wearing pale-blue silk pyjamas that matched his eyes and complemented his fair hair. He looked very young.

'Jordan. By the Red Sea. Rather a good hotel, this. It's on the beach. D'you fancy a shower? Shall I ring for breakfast?'

'No. Yes. I don't know.'

Barbara sank back against the pillows. She had never been so tired. In this state of mind and body what did it matter if she were seen taking breakfast in a bedroom in which there was also a man? After all, he was gay.

While Teddy sang in the shower Barbara pulled on the rest of her clothes. By the time he came out she was sitting at the table by the window drinking coffee and feeling a little better.

'You were very brave yesterday,' she said, as she passed him his cup. 'However did you know the girl would break down like that?'

'I didn't. It was a stupid thing to do, really. I could have got us both killed. But I've often been frightened myself, you see, most of my life, I suppose. So I could tell she was. Almost funny, isn't it? She wasn't a terrorist at all. She just wanted to see her boyfriend. You were very good, too: finding out she spoke some French, letting her talk, mopping her up, a shoulder to cry on.'

'I usually cope.' Confession did not come lightly to Barbara. She crumbled her roll, not hungry. 'That's what frightened me most. Perhaps my life has been too structured. I never allowed for surprise, for being out of control.' She managed a pale smile. 'Hijacks happened to other people. I know better now. I don't expect I'll learn. One doesn't, does one.'

After breakfast Barbara had a number of things to do. Once these were accomplished she joined Teddy on the beach. He was lying on a lounger in the shade of a parasol.

'I got hats for us both and bought you some sun-block,' she said. 'You're the burning type. I have also managed to get hold of a map and some not very helpful information.

Now, it appears that travel is not permitted between Jordan and Israel. Officially, they are still at war.'

'But isn't that Israel down the beach there?'

Teddy looked at his hat. It said PETRA.

'Yes. Eilat. And Egypt down there at the edge of the Sinai desert. And that way, Saudi Arabia.'

Teddy's tone was wistful.

'It's very beautiful.'

'Yes. So the long way would be a flight to Amman. Then Amman to Cairo, if the airport is open again. A bus from Cairo to Tel Aviv and a taxi to Jerusalem. I obtained these facts with the greatest of difficulty. I had never met Arabs before. They seem friendly but slow.'

'That would be the heat.'

Teddy read Barbara's hat. It said WADI RUM.

'Doubtless.'

Teddy yawned. A rather delightful lethargy had laid him flat on his back and it seemed a pity to sit up to look at Barbara's map. To his surprise, he liked it here. He liked Arabs and sun and this divine bay and the pink-washed desert hills and thinking of nothing.

But Barbara was probably right. One did not change in any basic or important way.

He knew he was expected to ask: 'So we should look for a short way to bypass the long way?'

'That's my conclusion. You see, here we are on the map. And there's Wadi Araba, a sort of no-man's-land between Eilat and Aqaba. And the Dead Sea, there.'

Teddy had been in a cold hell with Barbara. Now he imagined a very hot place.

'We could swim? The water's wonderful. Just swim out a bit and step ashore at Eilat?'

'Haven't you noticed the gunboats?'

'Ah. No. Is that what they are?' Teddy knew she was going to tell him, so he might as well ask: 'So how do you suggest we get there?'

'We walk.'

'All that way? In this heat?'

'We could probably find camels. There's one over there.

It gives rides to children. The females are best, I believe. Lawrence preferred them. They bite less and will run until they die.'

Now Teddy was sitting up straight. Barbara had his full attention.

'A camel?' he said. 'A dead camel?'

Daisy had come out looking for a taxi but it appeared that taxis in Jerusalem did not cruise. In the end Fedor had rung for one but there had been some difficulty. Also, Fedor clearly disapproved of her expedition.

'Miss Herbert, I wish you would not go.'

'Whyever not, Fedor?'

'Most people go from Ben Gurion or Dov. Tel Aviv. For Jerusalem airport you must drive through the West Bank. It is in the occupied territory.'

'So was Bethlehem. Nothing happened to me there.'

'You were lucky.'

'Don't worry, Fedor dear. I'll be fine.' Just as Daisy was leaving, she had remembered: 'And you won't forget, will you, Fedor? If Miss Banks arrives you don't know where I am or when I'll be back. After all, it's true.'

Daisy would have said that there was very little she was frightened of. Yet this drive into unmarked territory did slightly unnerve her. The driver was the same man whose cab she had taken a few days before. But if he was manic then, he was now in a depressive phase. The ashtray between the two front seats was crammed full with cigarette ends. He seemed disinclined to make conversation and drove too fast. Daisy saw, above the dashboard, a photograph of a woman with two children.

'Is that your family?'

'Yes.'

Daisy hung on or she would have been flung across the cab. She was not aware at what point they had crossed the line and entered the West Bank territory. Everything looked much the same: desert, scrub, small towns. No soldiers, no tanks, an empty road. Or not quite empty. In the ditch there, a burned-out car, abandoned.

The driver jerked his head.

'Ramallah.'

The crucifixion, Daisy remembered. She felt as she had before in this country, a fool, a naïve Englishwoman, an impertinent tourist. To her, Ramallah looked like just another hill town, more right in its place than the ugly cabins put up for the new settlers.

'Do you hate them?' she said. Over the brow of that small incline, an Arab, a figure from the Old Testament, was driving a herd of goats. Yet he looked neither to right nor left. He was passive in the landscape.

'I did. My children do. All the children have nightmares, Arab and Jew. Now I think, anything for peace, they are just people.'

He shrugged. What he meant was, don't ask me questions.

Apparently they had arrived. It didn't look like an airport but it must be. Daisy paid the taxi-driver and was working out the tip when he was off, gone, away.

No Jewish jokes today.

'Did you say Gnostics?' Eugenia said.

Fedor nodded. 'It says here they're staying at the King David.'

Eugenia was soaking offal in water. She dropped in the last bloody bit.

'Along with the Mormons and the Flat-Earthers and Anti-Resurrectionists; no doubt. Not to mention Jehovah's Witnesses, cholesterol-free dieters, futureologists and protestors against the Virgin birth. And missionaries crazy enough to imagine still that they can convert the Jews, that the world would be better should the Jews convert. Some perfectly sane people have believed that, you know. Any Essenes?'

'There's nothing here. What are Essenes?'

'I've never been quite clear. Dead Sea scrolls and all that stuff. Miss Mary sees them from time to time in Jericho. They were kind to her after her loss.' Eugenia stirred her unpleasant bowl with a wooden spoon. 'Well, at such times it is to be expected. It has happened before and it has always been the same: cranks, sects and schisms. The first thing that happens is fundamentalism and a lot of shouting. Then the fundamentalists fall out among themselves. So now you have Moslem against Moslem, Hamas fighting Fatah. Israeli peaceniks and Temple Faithful.'

'And there's an announcement here about a conference of vulcanologists and seismologists. It was going to be international but it's not now because of the emergency. Apparently the astrologers have been doing overtime because of the earthquakes.'

Fedor put down the newspaper. Eugenia settled in the basket chair in the sun. Everywhere in the house, and in the new air-raid shelter, she had nests of knitting. She kept stocking stitch for the kitchen.

'I wonder if the Peace Forest picnic is still on,' Eugenia said. 'Have we heard from Morgan Pooley?'

'Not lately. But he's probably in trouble because of the Garden Tomb business. And they were going to make it ecumenical this year. Solly was definitely coming.'

Eugenia nodded and dropped a couple of stitches. Not that it mattered.

'A nice boy, Morgan,' she said. 'If he is in trouble we must help him, Fedor.'

Fedor thought what a confusing person Eugenia must appear to those who did not know her well. That was, everyone in the world but for him might be unaware of the kindness of her heart.

He saw that she was tired, that her knitting was getting ravelled by Miss Mary's cat, that the joints of her fingers were swollen and winter was coming, that she was gallant. And he loved her greatly.

So it was that they had a rest in the middle of the morning, since the Little Daughters of Sorrow had gone away to pray for the return of Sister Angelica, and no guests were expected.

Fedor asked about the Gnostics and Eugenia told him.

'Cranks on most counts. But right in a few respects. They say gnosis – that is, to know yourself – is at the same time to know God, human nature, destiny. And that there is a spirit, with us always. For anyone to recognise if they have eyes to see. I suppose you could say, they hold intuition to be higher than reason.'

Fedor thought for a moment.

'As we love?'

'Yes, exactly like that.'

When Fedor got up he thought that Eugenia was wrong about the weather. The sun was still shining calmly from a cheerful sky.

'I must feed the carp,' he said.

And then he noticed that something extraordinary was happening to Miss Mary's magic quilt. Usually it stayed much the same for quite a long time. But today it was constantly changing from one blink to another, from a pattern of sun and flowers to birds to virgin white, then to a frenzy of confused and worried darker tones: black on white, red on black, blood. And all the birds had flown.

FIFTEEN

Eugenia was right. It would rain but not yet. Through the day, even while the sun shone, thunderheads assembled to the north-east: the same direction from which the great assault, if it happened, might come. Up there, the sky was heavy with rain, stretched tight beneath the weight of waters.

They would not spill yet, though. So the woman in blue, Miss Mary, wandering free in time and place and yet not without direction, rested for a time at Yad Vashem. She walked between the trees in the Avenue of the Righteous among Nations and thought, this killing, will there be no end to it?

Most came as tourists to this quiet place, the holocaust memorial, and left as penitents. Always in tears: for the Jews, for themselves, for how far they had all fallen from the angels they might have been.

Outside the Children's Memorial, by the statue of every mother who has ever wept for her child, Mary touched a man's hand, a woman's cheek, and both were comforted, although they could not have said why.

She paused under the trees near the entrance where kittens played. Then she knew she must hurry. With the first pain she caught her breath. It would not be long.

Daisy tried to hang on to consciousness and to remember what had happened, in order.

She recalled the taxi-driver and her arrival at the airport. Expecting a drama, she had found a small but clean waiting area, an elderly couple serving coffee and one security guard: a boy with the usual sub-machine-gun. A kitten was outstaring

161

the Uzi. The man who had checked Daisy in could not say when or if there would be a flight.

'Is it an emergency?'

'It is normal,' he said.

She talked to the cat. She saw from the window one Dash aircraft shunted off the runway and a couple of planes that looked military.

It was already close indoors and grew stuffier. The sky seemed to be sucking the air from the earth. The couple behind the counter were full of smiles. They wanted Daisy to have some good Israeli orange juice, a bag of bagel snacks, a newspaper. They spoke only Hebrew and Russian but it was clear that their intentions were kind.

Daisy smiled back and thought that it was good; these two were pleased with the life they had made here, it was more than enough for them. Here, they implied, their very existence suggested, you can sometimes burrow optimistically into dangerous and unpromising circumstances and make for yourself a modest bivouac.

Then, as the air began to shake with heat and no other passengers arrived and no plane took off, Daisy realised it was mid-afternoon. She was hungry and faint and the snack-bar had closed and she was in occupied territory on a fool's errand, in pursuit of a man she hardly knew, who might or might not have come this way. When she could have gone with Gideon to Jericho.

Now, the boy with the sub-machine-gun had reappeared and was saying that Daisy must go away. No flights today.

'The airport is to be evacuated.'

'But how do I get back to Jerusalem?'

He shrugged. Your problem, he meant. From the young, at least, courtesy was not an Israeli characteristic, Daisy had noted. Who could blame them? They were born to hate and distrust. Again she saw the eyes of the Palestinian prisoner on the way to Bethlehem: this is how it is, how I am.

Outside the terminal she shaded her eyes. There was a smack of gunfire. A figure was running across the road, zig-zag. From behind a white security van someone threw a grenade.

There must have been a taxi waiting, after all. The battered Citroën appeared to come from nowhere. It slid up beside her, the door open, and gratefully she got in. There was someone else, another passenger in the back seat. Daisy turned to speak to him and then she recalled nothing until she woke, swimming upwards to consciousness.

'Steady,' someone said.

Daisy tasted something foul in her mouth and throat. She opened her eyes and found herself exactly where she had wanted to be, in her right and proper place, if not in the circumstances she had envisaged, in Thomas's arms.

Kalfayan nodded as his former catamite made his report. He spat out a date stone and scratched his piles. They were always at their worst in this kind of weather: low and close. And the rash around his sexual organs was spreading up his body. It had reached the armpits and would doubtless soon join up with the pustules on his neck that made shaving so painful.

His eye beneath its patch stabbed as he watched the boy leave the lead-lined, well-furnished bunker beneath Ararat Street. Ah, the turn of those buttocks!

But the days of the downy boys were gone for ever, which should have been the greatest of anguishes. Yet perhaps there was something to be said, Kalfayan thought to himself, for enforced celibacy. It concentrated the mind, left the passions free to nourish his greater fervour, his crusade to strip naked the fools of the world. In a way, there might be something holy about his cause, monkish about his devotion.

Up to now he had kept clear of the hostage business. But then people were commodities, like everything else. The Beirut market was no longer bullish but if he couldn't sell them wholesale then he would do the retailing of the man and the girl himself. At the best, their loving families would pay up. At the worst, he could leave them where they were. They would become as dung in the long history of Jerusalem's dead. That was history: shit.

Kalfayan yawned. Though his mind blazed his body pulled him down, to sleep, perhaps to death. He burned

163

one moment, shivered the next. He called for his precious volume of medieval erotica but found himself no longer stirred by these wonderfully intricate and embellished engravings of Pope and Whore, Virgin and Ass.

His stalk had sickened and withered and what was the use of lust in the head?

I am dying, he supposed at last. Soon I shall have to test my own goods, the kindness of the needle.

And after all the deals are done and my eyes close on this world, will I be granted before my descent to hell, the grace of a last vision? If so, let it be the face of that boy I knew once in Marrakesh. He smelled of oil and sandalwood and his lips were sweet.

Hamida screeched.

'What are you doing? Take your hands off me! I shall go to my father's house!'

Hamil raised the slipper for the third time. He had never thought he could bring himself to do it but after the first thwack it had not been so difficult. The only real problem had been in getting Hamida across his knees and keeping her there. She was a well-fleshed woman and remarkably strong for someone who spent most of her days in the bedroom reading trash about film stars, eating sweets and drenching herself in her father's perfumes from heavy cut-glass sprays with gold tassels. It was there he had caught her, against her frilly pillows with her mouth full of chocolate.

'I love you!' he cried and brought down the slipper.

'I know where to get respect! You have gone mad!'

'Then you have driven me mad!'

'The neighbours will hear!'

'Let them!'

'My father will kill you!'

Thwack! Even though it was permitted in his faith, Hamil had never before thought of raising a finger to Hamida, any more than he had considered putting her away for her childlessness. Although to the outsider there might appear to be little to love in this fat, lazy, wailing woman, Hamil saw inside all this complaining blubber a girl with eyes the colour of caramel, a soft voice and beautiful buttocks that swayed beneath her skirts. Who cooked for him with her own hand, sending the maid away, his favourite laham baagine with lemons and yoghurt and kebbe fish; and herself fed him eggplant dip on pitta bread. This last had been a ceremony of special meaning to both of them for it led more often than not to the nibbling of finger-tips, the kissing of her small palm and love-making. In those early days neither could eat eggplant dip in company without smiling.

Thwack!

Hamil guessed that her failure to produce a child had turned Hamida away from love-making and into screeching, as he himself had turned away from her reproaches into sadness and silence and something like madness.

At last she had stopped thrashing and wriggling in her attempts to get free.

Hamil waited, slipper raised, for the next screech but nothing came. For a dreadful second he thought he had killed her. The slap of the slipper had been barely hard enough to hurt her flesh but perhaps the shock had stopped her heart? Or she had choked on chocolate?

He had heard the flinging open of their neighbours' shutters, a cock crowing in answer to her shrieks. In the small cul-de-sac where they lived Hamida's screams were a matter of daily entertainment. Hamil could sense now a listening silence. He imagined himself stepping out into the courtyard, as on to a stage, Hamida's lifeless corpse in his arms; he, inconsolable widower and murderer at once.

'Hamida,' he whispered and tears of remorse already pricked his eyes.

Then he realised it was not he but Hamida who was sobbing; at first dry gasps and then full-throated weeping.

He helped her to turn over and attempted to lay her comfortably against the pillows but she clung to him, howling against his shoulder. It was an extraordinary sound, such as comes in spring in the desert when an underground source bubbles from the rock and floods a wadi. It was a wonderful weeping, one he had never dreamed to hear, as the dead might make awaking.

'Hamil, forgive me.' At last she did rest against the bedhead and accept his handkerchief. 'You should put me away. I am a terrible woman.'

'Not terrible, my heart. Unhappy.'

'Barren!'

Hamida's eyes were blue rather than red from weeping. Once she had blown her nose she appeared to Hamil as beautiful as she had ever been.

'Of no importance,' he said. 'And who knows what Allah holds for us in store?'

He was about to kiss her when she put her finger on his lips.

'Wait,' she said.

With her robe half off her shoulders, Hamida left the room. Hamil lay back on the bed. He heard the refrigerator door close.

Then the slap of her mules.

'Close your eyes,' Hamida said. 'Open your mouth.'

Hamil did as he was told. He tasted pitta bread and eggplant dip. Then she was in his arms, all eleven stone of her. They squashed the chocolates unheeding as one loved the other, and both together, until they could hardly tell the difference between them.

A soft wind ruffled the surface of Lake Tiberias and then was gone to rattle the leaves of Galilee and Nazareth.

Then the air was still, but not to be trusted. The weather waited. So did the watchers on the Golan Heights and the Listeners in the City. The people searched the sky and hurried home, though it was not the weather they feared.

Nor was it the weather above that interested the Conference of seismologists as they read their readings and faxed their observations around the world.

Below Jerusalem, deeper than the most ancient of workings, older than man, there was a voice even the Listeners had not intercepted, as the earth itself complained.

Miss Mary's first pain had not been repeated. There was plenty of time after all, she decided, and panting a little,

166

settled for a rest at Bethany. From where she sat in the shade she could see the other Mary, and Martha, in their garden, gossiping while chickens ran around and a kitten stalked them. She thought of her own cat and smiled, thinking there was solace in such things. The small, the trivial, the exchange of stories, the soft-bee talk of women, the call of the collared-dove, a ripe handful of olives. After a while, she slept. And woke with the strangest sensation of falling, as if the earth had tipped.

Morgan thought, not for the first time, that there was an awful lot to be said for working your way through a list of small jobs, especially when there were a lot of big problems about which there was no point in worrying.

For instance, although it had been an awkward interview with the Bishop, not to mention the telephone call from the Garden Tomb Association in England, at least he had not lost his job. So although there might be a war any minute and Daisy was not in love with him nor he with her, and Barbara Banks was on her way to Jerusalem and the whole of the book she had commissioned was still in her head, and although the sky was blue there was a most peculiar feel in the air, as if one were about to be squashed by a descending ceiling and rising floor, at least there was the Peace Forest Picnic to be organised.

That is to say, there were all the usual telephone calls to be made, to guests, caterers and coach company, and in addition this year there was an interesting complication. The Bishop (or, more likely, Mrs Bish who ran her husband like a tight ship) had insisted on the ecumenical. So Morgan poured himself a large glass of Celebration Cream, telephoned fifty people, marked them all on his list with a tick, a cross or a question mark, and then listed in his small, neat hand the queries arising from the edict:

Armenians?
Lutherans?
Check Solly Herzog re prayers
Check Bish re prayers
No prayers?

167

Kosher chick no shellfish
Moslems??

Morgan crossed out the last item. They wouldn't come anyway and if they did it would be terribly embarrassing.

Morgan tapped his teeth with his pen. On the whole, it might be best to make the occasion strictly secular.

The Bish would want a few words to kick off, though. Something that implied celebration, Morgan considered, words fit to be spoken in that wonderful forest, the most miraculous greenness he had ever seen, a fine setting.

Morgan pondered. What one needed were words that could be spoken by any man of any faith, even the hopeful faithless. Then he remembered Job 38:7.

. . . when the morning stars sang together,
and all the sons of God shouted for joy.

Of course, in the present political situation there might be no picnic and certainly nothing to shout about. Still, Morgan had lived here long enough to know how trouble could be seen on the horizon, like a sandstorm in the desert, and have changed face or be gone by dawn.

In any case, although frequently fretful, Morgan inclined to optimism and he was pleased with his morning's work: his satisfaction completed by the sight of Sheba playing in the garden in the green light.

Then the cat stopped, twitched the end of her tail and quite suddenly bolted at the same moment that everything on Morgan's desk jiggled very slightly and then was still.

In the uncomfortable mini-coach thumping its way from Eilat on the Red Sea to Jerusalem, Teddy lurched awake and was nearly thrown from his seat. So too, it appeared, was everyone else. Even the three muscled and alarming Israeli young looked surprised.

'What was that?' Teddy said.

Barbara shrugged. Teddy had had his hour of glory in the air. He had basked in it for a while and would remember forever that he had once, at least, been brave. Now Barbara was coping again.

'Probably an earth tremor,' she said. 'Oh, look, there's the Dead Sea.'

Teddy looked. He decided that the Dead Sea was unattractive. It lived down to its name. Definitely shuddery. He closed his eyes again and wished he could forget the exhausting events of the last twelve hours. He could hardly believe that by night (though not, thank heaven, by camel) he and Barbara, in company with an expensive squinting Arab, had actually made their way by foot across the outstandingly unattractive no-man's-land between Jordan and Israel, dodging mines, surveillance systems and border guards. It was so dangerous it was supposed to be impossible. Teddy decided there must have been a miracle.

The desert night had been as bitterly cold as the day was ferociously hot. Barbara had conducted the negotiations with the brother-in-law of the squinter's cousin at the dirty end of Aqaba in a mixture of English and what Teddy assumed must be Arabic – a peculiar language that sounded like gargling.

The squinter was undoubtedly a Palestinian terrorist and even more certainly unreliable, so it could only have been by a miracle that they had somehow evaded Israeli eyes and ears and by six a.m. were eating breakfast in a four-star beach-fronting hotel in Eilat. They even had showers and a nap by the pool.

The airport, Barbara announced, was closed to civilian traffic, so instead, here they were at last on the road to Jerusalem.

It should have been a great moment but all Teddy wanted was sleep and, if not oblivion, then sweet dreams.

He was just settling down to winter in England and toast with Gentleman's Relish by the fire in Bedford Row, when he had to wake up and listen to Barbara, who was explaining something.

'You see, the great Rift Valley finishes round about here. That's one of the places where the earth doesn't join up properly.'

'Ah.'

Now Teddy was lying back on soft cushions on an English

summer river in a punt, shading his eyes with one hand at the tangled sun in the willows, when Barbara said: 'Oh, do look at that signpost. You must look.'

Teddy resolved, I will not, I shall not open my eyes.

'What does it say?'

'Sodom.'

'What was that?'

'What?'

'Things sort of moved. It's stopped now. Didn't you notice?'

'No.'

Thomas shook his head. He was smiling. He had been smiling ever since Daisy fell into his arms, flung through the door, half-fainting. And she had opened her eyes and he had said: 'Steady.'

Since then, since she recognised him, it seemed to Thomas that they had conducted a whole courtship in this tiny cell. Courtship, he had thought, what a good word for a ritual full of grace. A rite he found to his surprise, he was able instinctively to observe – as were they both – before the naming of it came to him.

At first there had been wonder, though Daisy had seemed less astonished, either by the finding of him or by love. Thomas thought, perhaps women knew better than men what would happen in the end. They were no more capable of influencing events but they moved in time to the earth. There came back to him the wonderful simplicity with which William (whose hand he had surely felt on his shoulder) spoke of his two loves; the one for the man in the Garden, the other for his wife in the English orchard in Kent. Love divine in both senses, the spirit and the flesh, the flashing threads tangled, two springs and one bright stream.

There had been no need to tell her to steady. She had simply opened her eyes and said: 'I was looking for you. I thought you'd gone to Sinai.'

'Someone whacked me on the head. Near the Garden Tomb. At night.'

'What were you doing there?'

'I imagined that might be where William had his vision. Doesn't seem to matter now, does it?'

'No.' Daisy opened those pale-lashed eyes. Thomas imagined the taste of her thin skin: some sharp herb. She looked at his lips, anticipating what it would be to kiss.

'They shoved some filthy pad over my nose and mouth,' she said. 'I can still smell it. I think there was shooting at the airport. How long have you been here?'

'I'm not sure.' Thomas was still holding Daisy. That is, he had not thought of letting go, but, having helped her to her feet, was standing with his arms around her. While they talked their bodies were having a quite separate conversation. His hand was wanting to learn the feel of Daisy's hair – the fox-colour at the moment dull with dust.

But he said: 'You'd better sit down. Here, let me help you.'

'What's going to happen to us? Is there any way out of here?'

No longer touching, their bodies were suddenly shy.

'There's a cleft above us, where the light is, but no way through,' Thomas said. 'And that could be the beginning of a tunnel down there. But it's too low. I don't see a way in. I don't suppose you have anything to eat or drink?'

'Yes, I have! Here in my bag – fruit sweets. Suck them slowly. We'd better start with one each. When I couldn't find you Fedor let me into your room and I read William's journal. That's why I thought of Sinai.'

'I was going a bit mad before you came. I even thought William was here. And someone else. And then those olives came from nowhere.'

'I expect he was here,' Daisy said. 'D'you remember walking back to Madame Muna's after Morgan Pooley's party? You wouldn't look at me. You were going to be a monk.'

Thomas unhooked his long legs from under his chin and stretched them. He could just touch the opposite side of the cave.

'Ah. Yes. I was running away from something. Or towards. Not sure which. I've got to get you out of here. I suppose our only hope is to clobber the next person to open the door. But we've no weapon. Not even a stone, just pebbles.'

'I saw something in Gethsemane,' Daisy said. 'And then there was a boy, Jibreel. You know they crucified an Arab on the road to Ramallah? If we put all the pebbles into one of your socks, that would be just as good as a stone.'

'That's a brilliant idea.' Thomas could not run away even if he had wanted to but his train of thought was as jerky as ever. 'I don't know if you saw it but William made a last entry in his journal. When he was back in Kent but about those four years in Jerusalem after Sinai. He wrote: "I went again to the Garden and He was not there." And yet I'm certain about that vison. I believe it.'

'You'd better take your socks off.'

He had such thin wrists and long, white feet.

Daisy said: 'I think I recognised you the first time I saw you. At the airport.'

'Did you? Really?'

Now, at last, they turned their heads to face each other, and the dim filtered light from the Holy Sepulchre above was more than enough for mouth to find mouth and reason to fall asleep and speech be stopped

'It's not exactly raining but the air's wet,' Fedor was saying. He and Eugenia had gone to bed early. There had been no one for dinner. Sister Angelica had rung to say she was not coming back but converting to anything that seemed promising, so the Little Sisters of Sorrow had left in a delicious flurry of tears, scandal and godless chatter on the last coach to Ben Gurion, whence they would fly, if necessary on white starched wimples, high and away.

'Good riddance,' Eugenia said. 'Where's the vodka?'

'But I am a bit worried,' Fedor continued, 'about Miss Herbert and Thomas Curtis. He's left his shaving things and Jerusalem airport's closed. So why didn't she come back?'

'Doubtless for reasons of her own,' Eugenia said. 'She is a resourceful young woman. They are in love. They may have found each other.'

'All the same. They've just said on the radio there's been

an earth tremor. And that's not all. The Holy Sepulchre was singing. Solly says Gideon's been recalled to his unit and that cousin of Miss Herbert's rang from Eliat. Miss Herbert asked me to say she wasn't here and she isn't so I could. But she sounds very determined. And Morgan Pooley asked us to the Peace Forest Picnic. What with everything, I'm surprised they're having it.'

'Fedor, dear, you are going on. I think you must be tense.'

'Are we going to the picnic?'

'Of course. We always do. When people are worried that is precisely the time to have a picnic.' Eugenia delved into her knitting bag. Her spectacles slid to the end of her nose. 'That cat of Miss Mary's has gone off with my angora. I wonder if it's pregnant. Do settle down, my darling. Perhaps you're trying too hard to remember again? You haven't been thinking about the abattoir?'

Fedor shook his head. Eugenia pushed her spectacles back up her nose to look at him.

'Here, let me rub your shoulders. You're all knotted. That's better. Now rest your head, here.' Fedor lay, his head on Eugenia's breast outside the knitted bed-jacket. Still, he could hear her heart beating and it was in time with his.

Eugenia stroked his brow.

'Did I ever tell you about Simon Magus?' She had but Fedor sometimes thought that the best stories are those that are told again and again. Certainly they were the best to hear in bed and to go to sleep with. So he closed his eyes and listened. And Eugenia recounted again, as she had before, what a wonderful sight it had been (and would, accordingly, be again): the Samaritan magician who tried to buy Christianity from St Peter, flying around the domes and spires of Rome.

'But he flew too high and broke his ankle falling. My father always said he was a charlatan. I liked him, but, of course, all children love magicians because they believe in magic. Are you asleep yet, my love?'

'Not quite. Almost.'

'I think we might cook the carp quite soon. They are said in Urfa to be poisonous but that is not true.'

173

'But the Indian story? That they hold souls for safe keeping? Wouldn't that make us cannibals?'

'Less than the taking of the Eucharist, if you believe in that. In any case, however often they are eaten, still they remain. That is the magical thing about them. My great-great-grandfather told my great-grandfather who told my father. And my nurse told me.'

Fedor's voice was drowsy.

'Tell me your nurse's story again. How many virgins did it take to make the golden net?'

'I think it was fifty.'

Eugenia smiled. Fedor slept.

In the small hours of the morning Jerusalem was shaken awake.

Those who sheltered in the deep caves were afraid to stay and afraid to leave. If they could. Terror was from above but also all around.

Daisy and Thomas were disturbed in their loving, their eyes and mouths filled with dust in an imitation of death.

Kalfayan swore. Flung from his bed, he called for a candle and his servant to slap.

'Where is the candle?'

'Here.'

'I cannot see it.'

'Master, that is because you are blind.'

Hamil and Hamida did not realise what was happening as the earth moved, such love they had been making.

Fedor sat up.

'What was that?'

'An earthquake. Nothing to do with us.'

But Fedor was pulling on his slippers.

'The cat will be frightened.' He hung on to the bed. It had settled again and the dresser was returning to the horizontal.

'Is that the bell?'

It was confusing because whatever had happened had set off every bell in Jerusalem ringing as if for the second coming.

But then he felt sure. Someone was banging at the kitchen door.

'Perhaps you had better go.' Eugenia was wide awake now. That was her softest time, when she had just woken from sleep.

'You know who it is, don't you?' Fedor reached for his trousers.

'Yes. I think I do.'

The electricity was off. The after-shudders of the quake made Fedor feel like a sailor who has lost his land-legs. He finally found a candle and lit it. Jerusalem was no stranger to power-cuts.

Then he unlocked the door and before the wind blew out the candle-flame he saw who it was. He knew the face and the colour of the robes.

'Help me, Fedor. I think I'm falling. Thank you, your hand.'

'Miss Mary! Please come in. Come in.'

SIXTEEN

S till, the rain held off. The weather waited while the not-so-solid earth grumbled and settled, although some-times in new configurations.

Crusaders, Jews and Moslems stirred in their sleep. Armour clanked. Tears ran from dead eyes. Some reached for arms.

The dead who had been planted in preferential graves outside the Golden Gate (first in the queue for heaven), sat up in their winding sheets.

'Is this the Day of Judgement?'

'Not yet. Lie down.'

'Is it war again?'

'Not this time.'

Many had not slept at all. Others had rude awakenings.

Within sight of Jerusalem itself, two things had happened to annoy Barbara Banks. The mini-coach had broken down and there had been an earthquake, or, rather, a second shock, high enough on the Richter scale to be beyond even Barbara's coping.

If he had not been fond of her by now and himself exhausted, Teddy would have found it hard not to laugh. Poor Barbara, torn between anger and alarm, obliged to defer to those ferocious young sabras who insisted that they all sleep out of doors.

'Why?' said Barbara, clutching her sponge-bag.

'Because it's the safest place in an earthquake,' Teddy explained.

They tramped over a rutted field between olive trees. The driver had vanished, apparently dissolved. The young Israelis

176

lit a fire as though they did this every night. Then they sang.
Then they danced.

Barbara shivered. Teddy wrapped his coat around her.

'Why don't you lie down? Put your head in my lap.'

So she did. And then she sat up again.

'I have a terrible feeling I'm going to cry,' she said. And
then, drowsily: 'You're a nice man, Teddy. I quite wish you
weren't gay.' She accepted his large handkerchief, sniffed and
dabbed her eyes. 'Where are we, anyway?'

'Bethlehem.'

With the exception of Magdalena's bar and Madame Muna's
guest-house, both of which were miraculously exempt from
history and natural disaster, nowhere in the ancient City was
safe. Not even King Solomon's quarries nor Hezekiah's tunnel; nor Kalfayan's shelter, where the now blind Armenian,
mocked and abandoned by his servants, had almost but not
quite given way to despair.

If he had not forgotten how, he would have wept. Instead,
he turned his inner eye to the map of Jerusalem's entrails and
bowels he held inside his skull. He would sleep and then he
would discover how much remained, if there were any way
up or out.

Meanwhile Kalfayan sampled his own wares. As day broke
he was still adrift in the sleep of the divine poppy.

Eugenia woke, opened her eyes, found the world to be
unusually good, kissed Fedor awake and had pulled on her
lopsided star-coat before he had even decided who and where
he was.

'Find the fish-kettle, my darling,' she said, 'and catch
the carp.'

The epicentre of the second, fiercer shock, was below the
Holy Sepulchre, where, if Daisy and Thomas had not already
been in each other's arms, they would have been flung
together.

They had forgotten about braining the guard with a sockful
of pebbles – there was so much to talk about.

The talking itself had been a way of loving, everything they discovered about each other amazing, revelatory, most precious.

It was Daisy who had said, after that first kiss, 'No, wait.'

'Why?'

'I want to know you.'

'So do I.'

'I mean, first. Before.'

They found they could kiss and talk. So they were grazing one upon the other and marvelling at the fact that both were orphans, when the floor of the cave leaped, flinging Thomas upon Daisy and earth in both their eyes.

Thomas was the first to surface. What felt like a block of stone was on his back but he heaved it away with a strength that surprised him. Even the glimmer of light from above had gone and they were in utter darkness.

And so in darkness and blindness, they moled their way towards each other. Daisy thought she had lost her sight until she felt the earth all upon her. Thomas flailed with his arms where he guessed she should be, discovered her shape, called her name and dug frantically, as though for his own life. But then, she was his life.

He uncovered her face first. She was breathing and conscious. She choked and spat until he had her sitting, moaning his name, while Thomas hushed her. By feel, he dug until she was all free and then, so far as he could, wiped her face with a rag torn from his shirt.

Daisy clung to him, shaking with shock. Perhaps because of the utter darkness, they half-whispered, like children who have been put to bed and told not to talk.

'Hush,' he said, and rocked her. 'Shush. Anything broken?'

'Don't think so.'

Gently, by touch alone, Thomas found her long neck, the small bones of her face, her breasts; he stroked her poor face, her dusty hair, kissed the dirt from her lips, tasted her.

'No, you,' Daisy said. In her turn, she mapped his sharp

178

cheekbones, the narrow lines of his skull, his long hands, learning them. She kissed his torn knuckles. There was something about this coming to life, this blind knowing. 'Your face is bleeding. I thought we were dead.'

'No, just born. I wonder if we're under the Temple Mount. That's where the Lord formed man from dust. According to Genesis.'

Daisy smiled shakily. 'Well, they were right about the dust. So what do we do now? I wouldn't have minded so much before but now I don't want to die.'

'I think I did want to die. Or, rather, I wanted to put away myself. I envied William so much. That vision. To lose oneself, all that.'

Daisy wiped dirt from her mouth with the back of her hand and tasted Thomas's blood. 'This is an absurd conversation. We could still die here. I'm afraid we probably will.'

In that second she saw with a third eye, as though from a window in eternity, their two bodies curled together in this small cell, the flesh fall away, the bone crumble to dust, until all that was left was a tracing of their love, a relict in relief on the cave floor from which it was impossible to distinguish which of the two mingled forms was which; only that they had been human and they had loved.

Which was probably the best you could say of anyone.

According to the radio, the battle was off and peace was on. For the moment, thought Fedor, until the next time, his mind wandering as Eugenia consulted her Elizabeth David.

'Carpe à la Juive. How interesting, I'd forgotten. It's from *La Cuisine Messine*, nineteenth-century recipes from Lorraine.'

Fedor wondered aloud: 'Don't you think we ought to notify someone about Miss Herbert and Thomas Curtis? I mean, with the earthquake.'

Eugenia looked over her spectacles.

'I have told you there is nothing to worry about. And there will be no one to notify. They are all too busy digging each other up. It's surprising they have the power back on. Now, this really is quite simple. Olive oil, onions, flour, white sugar, water, wine vinegar, Malaga raisins and a quarter of a pound of skinned sliced almonds. That would be for one fish, so we'd better double it. Serve cold.'

'Do you think the new peace conference will come off?'

'In a pig's eye.' Eugenia frowned. 'No Malaga raisins. We'll have to make do. Can't believe it matters. She doesn't seem very keen on it as a dish. But that's not the point. I have never approved of gourmet food – all those nervy palates twitching and fussing.'

Fedor blinked. Last night Miss Mary had come in on a great wind but the air again was a coffin-lid.

'What about the fifty virgins?'

'What virgins?'

'To catch the carp. And the golden net.'

'Fiddle. That lepidopterist, Nabokov, left a butterfly net strong enough to catch a flying shark. It's under the stairs with the cricket bat. Fedor, my dear, you're still very nervy. I have a feeling you are trying too hard to remember.'

'Perhaps I am.'

'You will never remember until you forget.'

'I expect you're right. I'd better take Miss Mary her breakfast.'

'Fish first. Then Miss Mary. She's still asleep, worn out, poor soul. She must be very close to her time. I'm glad she found her way home.'

'What's the matter with her?' Fedor worried. 'I do hope she's not ill.'

'Only as ill as any woman might be in her ninth month.'

'But she hasn't been away for nine months.'

'No. But who knows in what circle of time she chose to move or found herself?'

Fedor nodded.

'So there'll be a baby?'

'Obviously. A son who will doubtless bring trouble in the end, as he did before.' Eugenia looked up from her cookery book. 'But also some comfort and joy. Good tidings, as the carol says. Have you seen the wine vinegar?'

'Who's going to eat the fish, anyway?'

'Why, the three of us, of course. You, Miss Mary and I.'

Through the day, all the time the carp was cooking and cooling, Jerusalem licked her wounds and counted her dead, of which there were remarkably few. Many of those taken to hospital had mistaken the quake for an attack and given themselves the antidote for nerve gas. Others thought the big bomb had been dropped and had to be coaxed from their cellars. The seismologists and vulcanologists were gleeful with their measuring and their noting. The archeologists despaired.

The animals had been the most frightened. Morgan Pooley had lost his cat. The dogs still howled. The bells were cracked.

Eugenia put the fish to settle into its own cooking juice and arranged the almonds and raisins around it.

In Manger Square Barbara stamped her foot.

'I insist on transport to Jerusalem.'

The security policeman yawned and picked his nose.

Teddy sat in the only bar that was open, drinking mint tea with honey. He found himself surprisingly content. He was worried about the earthquake and what had happened to Thomas, naturally. But he had begun to think that, if the road to Jerusalem were so difficult, perhaps he was not intended ever to reach it. He would only be disappointed. It could not really be golden.

In her empty courtyard by the fig tree, Magdalena yelled back at the mynah bird shrieking in the bar, and looked up at the sky. If only it would rain. Then the first fat drop fell on her upturned face like a blessing.

Thomas suddenly realised that he could make out Daisy's bruised features.

'Look! Isn't that light? Not where it was before. Down there. There's been an earth-slip. That's a tunnel. And the air's fresh. Come on! I can smell rain.'

Fedor and Eugenia lay in their bed high above time. That first forgiving drop of rain had been followed by a downpour

181

like redemption, washing the streets clean, the Holy places, laying the dust. Unlike the thunderstorm, this rain was a prayer answered. It bowed Miss Mary's moon-flowers by their grateful heads and the overflowing waters flooded the pools of Hezekiah and Bethseda and the Sultan, and Madame Muna's carp-pool.

Fedor heard the rain and sat up straight in bed.

Eugenia murmured sleepily: 'What is it, my dear? The carp? Rather dull, I thought, but a good dinner. A spot too much rouge, perhaps? We should have had white.' Then she was wide awake. 'It's not that, is it? You're remembering?'

'Yes!'

'After the abattoir and the tea dances and the *calèche*? Tell me, then, what happened.'

'You know.'

'Yes, I do.'

Eugenia took his hands and kissed them. Fedor wondered, however could he have forgotten that the consummation he had so wished was already accomplished, years and years ago, in Cairo, after he had cradled Eugenia's instep and taken her hand. And she had led him to her bed, where they had stayed, for seven days and seven nights. And might still be there, given Eugenia's way with time. Or eternity's way with both of them.

Then he lay down. They lay together. Eugenia's hands were knotted, her feet cold, and Fedor was no longer so young, either.

All the same it was better even than it had been in Cairo, slower and more tender and then passionate beyond all senses in which the word is understood, as Fedor and Eugenia made what is commonly called love.

And the magic quilt was changed again. The birds returned but as part only of a larger pattern in which a hundred hearts were entwined, beating as one.

Thomas and Daisy, redeemed, restored, forgiven, stumbled out into the night and raised their faces and opened their mouths to drink the heavenly rain.

At the same moment Eugenia, waking from a deep dream

in which she and Fedor swam in her father's pool, flank to flank with the golden carp, woke Fedor.

'What is it?' He was seized by a remembered fear. 'Is it the end of the world?'

'No, quite the opposite. Miss Mary's waters have broken.'

'So what happens?'

'You put the kettle on, Fedor, my dear. And everything begins again.'

SEVENTEEN

The day of the Peace Forest Picnic was one of ripe apples falling from the bough, of Indian summer: everything suffused with gold, from the dome of the Mosque of Omar to Daisy's foxy hair.

With Sheba come home, Morgan had started the day in good spirits, up since six o'clock chasing caterers, revising the placement in the coach. He knew only too well that ecumenicism – the fantasy of a broad church holding many mansions – was one of those nice ideas thought up by Anglicans when they felt lonely. It was not for nothing that the Apostles were said to have spoken in tongues: the miraculous glossolalia that could be understood by all the clamorous children of Babel. Now the Roman Catholic charismatics were at it again, even though it must be perfectly clear that no one, with the possible exception of God, could make sense of a single word. There had been a time when Morgan was drawn by the RCs. Such theatre was appealing. But ultimately, he knew himself to be irredeemably English, middle church, and allergic to incense.

And so he had done his best to explain to everyone that secularism was to be the keynote of the picnic: just a few friends and acquaintances out on a modest spree.

Not that it would work like that, he knew. Already, only ten minutes on their short journey from the Jaffa Gate to the Peace Forest, the Armenians and the Greeks and the Russians were arguing with each other about whether or not to have the window open and the blind down or up. The Jewish children were running up and down the aisle under the eyes of their indulgent mothers, annoying the nuns.

Even among the Jews there were sects and schisms which

became immediately obvious once the coach had stopped its winding and climbing and put them all down at the picnic site, high in the clear air among the miracle of the trees.

'Oh dear,' Morgan said to Daisy. 'I thought we might have problems between the Ashkenazim and the Sephardics. But I never thought Mea Sharim would accept.'

'Who are they?'

'The ones you see at the Wailing Wall, with frock-coats and ringlets. Even the ordinary Israelis don't like them. If you drive through their quarter on the Sabbath you get stoned. They refused to travel with the rest of us so they had to have their own mini-coach. They insisted on interviewing the cook and now they won't sit with anyone else.' Even though it was only mildly warm, Morgan fanned his face with his white linen panama. 'If only Solly Herzog were here.'

'Yes.'

That had been a shadow on the outing. Last night they had heard that Gideon Solomon was reported missing, presumed dead, on the Golan Heights.

Thomas took Daisy's arm and they walked away from the site, up to a clearing which gave them a fine view of the hills and the picnic site with its white chequering of tablecloths, and a chance to be alone.

'About Gideon,' Thomas said.

Daisy shook her head.

'Apart from anything else, it would have meant taking sides. You can't live here properly, I mean married, any other way. You know his friend the imam told Fedor it was that Arab boy, Jibreel, who was crucified near Ramallah. I looked up his name. It means the faithful spirit or the bearer of revelation.' She was working things out for herself as much as she was telling Thomas. 'The two deaths, they don't cancel each other out. The balance compounds the horror.'

'And your ghosts?'

'Morgan told me, I'd forgotten. One of the early Churches believed that Christ could come to you in any form you recognise. I did see something in the Garden. And in Jibreel. Does that sound mad?'

'No. Ask William.'

Daisy touched a crisped leaf, golden. It crumbled between her fingers.

'You see, I think it's like the hymn or is it a prayer? If there is a god, he's *in* us. In our heads and in our understanding. Is that how it goes? What I mean is, we are god.'

'Maybe. I love you.'

'I know.' Daisy smiled. 'Look at them all down there. Are you hungry?'

'Not a bit.'

Thomas took her in his arms and they lay down on the forest floor and made love slowly.

Then they rested. And then they talked and Daisy touched the wounds on Thomas's face. They were still full of wonder, one for the other, and for what was between them.

After all, war did not break out. There was some kind of magic or blessing on the picnic. As the sun climbed to its meridian and then sloped down there was quiet talk, and sleep, and some understandings were made.

Barbara Banks, who had arrived in a fury and a downpour two nights ago, forgot why she had come. She liked Daisy's young man and formed a particular attachment to Eugenia Muna, who was instructing her in the mysteries of knitting. A pity Madame Muna couldn't be here today but it seemed there had been a birth.

Barbara thought she would like to come back here in the spring. This was a remarkable greening, exactly as Isaiah had foretold. And she was so enchanted by the young Morgan Pooley she could not bring herself to nag him about the commission he had clearly not started. There would be some way of cooking the books to write off the advance.

The young Pooley meanwhile was having a revelatory encounter behind Barbara's back with Teddy Short. They met by a famous grave of a dead musician who had trespassed against Judaic rites, that his ashes might be buried in the Land. Pilgrims dropped stones upon his sleeping-place in memory of ancient desert deaths, when jackals sought out those covered only by shifting sands.

Morgan and Teddy recognised each other at once. Shyly

at first. Then they talked and understood and knew they must be careful, for this might be love.

Then a high jet slashed the sky, reminding everyone that this was the real world of telegrams and anger. They were not exactly driven from the forest. Anyone who lived in this cockpit of history was acquainted with shock and familiar with grief, beyond surprise. All the same, someone stole a chicken, an Armenian nun concealed a smoked salmon under her robe, the arguments started up again, the tired children whined and some got slapped.

And there were those who looked behind them as the coach negotiated the bends going down, wryly, a little sadly, as if this were another garden and they were the ghosts of those first exiles, fleeing before a flaming sword.

That evening at dusk the blind Armenian left the Old City within the walls by the Zion gate, unremarked in a battered, dirty Citroën with the curtains drawn.

For the first time she could remember, Magdalena had climbed the steps to Madame Muna's guest-house. She did not stay long but she had heard of a child born and, meeting Fedor at the gate, left a sprig of myrrh from Jericho.

In Gethsemane the three Messiahs yawned. The one who wore the skull-cap on his bald head took it off, rubbed his pate and put it on again. He was beaming.

The other two turned.

'You've remembered!'

'Yes.'

'So what did Moses mean when he whispered to Joshua?'

'Well, you know he had a stutter?'

'Yes.'

'And he said take them to Ca–Ca–'

'Get on with it. What did he mean? Canaan?'

'No! My soul, what do you think he meant?'

They shook their heads again. It was no use rushing him.

'Where everyone wants to be! California!'

Magdalena was back in good time to open the bar. It was dark by the time the three friends had settled around the Crusaders' game-board. Not that any of them seemed inclined to play, even though it was a warm night for the time of year and the stars were brilliant.

Everything had been turned upside-down tonight. Solly, who was usually the soul of the party, was down. Fedor was up and so, even more unusually, was Hamil, the minor imam.

Magdalena came out with a cloth over her arm and a tray balanced delightfully on her hip. Tonight, regardless, she had brought angels' pee for everyone.

'Solly,' she said. 'I'm sorry.' She kissed him on the top of his head. 'It is terrible. It is so very sad.'

'Thank you, my dear. He was a good boy, a very good boy. We must tell ourselves it is just a small thing in the weave of a great carpet. Like the fault your people include always, Hamil, for fear of imitating the perfection of your god. I have wept already. But for a short time I wished for the company of my friends.' Solly swallowed his drink in one gulp and Magdalena fetched a refill. He seemed to think and to reach a conclusion. He nodded to himself and then his arms were spread wide as ever, as though to embrace.

'So, Hamil, I hear Hamida is pregnant?'

Hamil could not conceal his smile.

'So we are blessed. Inshallah.'

'And she is a good wife to you again?'

'She is my dove. Or, rather, we are two doves together. For which I must thank you, my friend.'

Solly waved his hand. His glasses gleamed, reflecting the candle and the moon.

'Nothing to do with me. It is yourself you must bless. And Fedor? I hear there is a child. A remarkable woman, Miss Mary.'

Fedor nodded. He felt happy about almost everything at the moment.

'And her cat has had kittens. It had made a nest in Eugenia's knitting wool. Angora. I can't help wondering if the carp brought it on.'

'The kittens? You feed your cats carp?'

'No. Miss Mary. I hadn't even realised she was pregnant.'

188

Fedor blushed unseen. 'I hadn't thought it was possible. I mean, given her age. Not that I know her age.'

'Haven't you realised yet? All things are possible.'

'I think I'm beginning to understand.'

Secretly, Fedor had been hoping that with so many wonders come to pass, this might be the night that Solly revealed the Byzantine gambit.

But that had been a selfish idea, Solly had a terrible grief to bear. It appeared that happiness never came quite unqualified. Eugenia, for instance, was not at all pleased that peace and the new child, along with media attention and wild rumour, had brought pilgrims, cranks, the lost, the forsaken, the longing, to the gates of her guest-house. All wanted the same thing: to see the child, or, failing that, to know its name.

Apparently, there was to be no chess. The three friends drank and Magdalena sat down and joined them. Fedor shifted very slightly. He was still not quite proof against that musk.

'Well?' said Magdalena, after a while. 'Are you going to tell us or not?'

She was addressing Fedor.

'You mean the end of the story?'

'Yes,' said Solly. Hamil wagged his long chin. The mynah bird shrieked. Magdalena yelled: 'Shut up or I'll stuff you! Get on with it, then.'

Fedor felt shy but he told them all of it, even the end, from the sight of Eugenia's instep in Cairo to the cooking of the carp. And approximately what followed.

When he had finished they were all quiet, except for a sigh of satisfaction.

It might have ended there but Solly was too sharp for him.

'There's something else, isn't there? To do with the fish?'

Sometimes Fedor felt that Solly knew everything, he could walk around inside your head as if he were in his own home.

'Well. Yes. What happened was, the morning after we had caught, cooked and eaten the fish, I went to look for Miss Mary's cat and they were still there. I mean, in the pool.'

Solly murmured: 'The sacred carp of Urfa. Of course. They will always swim.'

'For ever?'

'Yes. For ever.'

'A good story,' Magdalena sighed happily, 'and a good ending. Because it has no ending.' She stood, in that old, immortal posture, a hand on a swayed hip. A ripe fig fell from the tree of time. 'Right, gents,' she said, 'what'll it be? Same again?'